DEATH OF A PRIMA DONNA

Brina Svit

DEATH OF A
PRIMA DONNA

Translated from the Slovene by
Peter Constantine

THE HARVILL PRESS
LONDON

First published as *Smrt Slovenske Primadone*
by Založba Mladinska knjiga, 2000

2 4 6 8 10 9 7 5 3 1
Copyright © Editions Gallimard and Brina Svit, 2000
English translation copyright © Peter Constantine, 2005

First published in Great Britain in 2005 by
The Harvill Press
Random House, 20 Vauxhall Bridge Road,
London SW1V 2SA

Random House Australia (Pty) Limited
20 Alfred Street, Milsons Point, Sydney,
New South Wales 2061, Australia

Random House New Zealand Limited
18 Poland Road, Glenfield,
Auckland 10, New Zealand

Random House South Africa (Pty) Limited
Endulini, 5A Jubilee Road, Parktown 2193, South Africa

The Random House Group Limited Reg. No. 954009
www.randomhouse.co.uk

A CIP catalogue record for this book
is available from the British Library

ISBN 1 84343 045 2

Papers used by Random House are natural, recyclable products made from
wood grown in sustainable forests; the manufacturing processes conform
to the environmental regulations of the country of origin

Designed and typeset in Galliard by Palimpsest Book Production Limited,
Polmont, Stirlingshire

Printed and bound in Great Britain by
Mackays of Chatham

DEATH OF A PRIMA DONNA

Finally, I would like to add this short note for you to read at the beginning. As you see, I have answered all your questions concerning the Slovenian prima donna. I will admit that until the very last moment I was not sure whether I would. In fact, what made me decide to go ahead was the way certain questions were worded, as for instance: ". . . her great affection for home and family, particularly her mother" . . . "her return home, even at the height of her glory". Or: "She kept a special place in her heart for Ljubljana" . . . But also because of Lieutenant-Colonel Andreas Haas's point, that writing things down can have beneficial effects, such as distancing ourselves from events we no longer want to live with, or eradicating feelings of guilt.

From what I understand, your magazine is on its annual quest for Slovenia's Woman of the Year. But the year 2000 is a special year and this year's search has to be a special one, etc. (Here at *Petronius* we have planned a similar quest: the perfume of the century, the dress of the century, the wine of the century). "For this reason, Monsieur," you wrote to me, "the choice has to match the special occasion", adding that your group of collaborators would be wider than usual. Slovenia's Woman of the Century cannot have any secrets, you wrote. We want to know everything about her: her successes and failures, the loves of her life, both major and minor, anecdotes, memories. Even the most insignificant details you can recall, details that each of us could recognise in ourselves, will help us choose among our five finalists. Our prima donna, you said, has made it to the final round, together with a poetess, a long-distance runner, a social worker, and a television celebrity. And, you added, she is one step away from being Slovenia's Woman of 2000 – your answers will help her take that step.

If I were asked to do this again, I would probably refuse. But what's done is done. Before me lies a pile of writing to which I've given the title *The Slovenian Prima Donna*. Night is slowly dissolving: in an hour or two it will be gone.

As you will notice, I have not answered the questions in the order you asked them, although I have more or less answered them all. I only kept your order of questions at the beginning (What is your most pleasant memory of her? Your first interview? What really happened with the roses?) and at the end (Have you gone back to Slovenia? Are you sure you haven't forgotten to tell us something that might clinch her position as Slovenia's Woman of 2000?). In between, I have arranged my answers so that I can follow our story through to its end. What happened to her during these last few years, and also what happened between her and me, can in fact be called a story, because among other things it does have an ending.

Some questions that had to do with opera – such as, "Puccini or Janáček?" – I did not answer. That's the province of Lluis Toronto, the Catalan director, and others like him. He is about to publish his diaries dealing with his recent opera productions, in which the Slovenian prima donna is the central figure.

As you will see, I myself have raised many other questions, concerning Pablo Ortez and Julijan Remek, also Madame Ingrid. We always ask ourselves the real questions, which doesn't mean to say that we are able to answer them.

I

It was midwinter, on a hill just outside Ljubljana, in other words virtually in the city. One of those freezing afternoons when one would rather be lying under the covers staring up at the ceiling. But not Madame Ingrid. Madame Ingrid always does what she sets her mind to. In this case, take her two daughters out for some fresh air. She dressed them warmly – hats, gloves, boots – and drove them to the nearby hill. On the path through the woods she put the youngest down on the ground: the little girl traipsed through the snow, scooping it up in her arms. The older girl, Lejka, walked in front.

This memory, which with time has become mine, begins here. Lejka, walking along a narrowing path and hearing her sister's babbling and her mother's footsteps behind her. Lejka, also scooping up the fresh snow that sticks to her gloves and begins melting on her sleeves around her wrists. Lejka, throwing herself into the snow from time to time and then studying her imprint. That's me, that's me, that's me, she shouts every time. Not a soul to be seen. The sky is low and looks like a thick blanket of fog. The snow has changed the face of the forest. Lejka plods through the virgin snow and looks at the footprints she leaves behind. Then her hands begin to feel the chill. Of course: her gloves are wet, and stiff with cold. She tries to warm them with her breath. But the cold seeps even deeper. She takes off her gloves, puts them in her pocket, and pulls the sleeves of her woollen jacket down over her hands as best she can. It's no use, she feels the cold even more. Her fingers become yellowish and white. How can one's hands feel so cold? How can the cold hurt so much? She begins to look around. Ingrid and Lejka's little sister look tiny among the fir trees. Slowly, very slowly, they begin to grow, slowly she begins to differentiate their faces. My hands are cold, she shouts from a distance, they're cold and they hurt . . . When she reaches Ingrid, she notices through her tears that Ingrid looks worried. Ingrid bends down to her. What have you done? Can't you be more careful? Can't I trust you? she shouts, clasping Lejka's little hands tightly in hers. No, no, please, Lejka sobs. Hush, Ingrid commands. Ingrid massages her frozen hands. Then she puts them in her mouth. Both little hands suddenly into her warm mouth. Lejka falls silent, she tries to pull them out. No, no, she sobs. Ingrid grabs her wrists even tighter. Lejka closes her eyes and gives a long sigh. Oh, oh, why does it hurt so much . . .

But slowly she begins to feel warm and soft in her mother's mouth. Mmmm. The tears are still flowing down her cheeks, even though she no longer feels cold. Her fingers come back to life and feel the warm walls of mother's mouth, her hard, rough tongue, and the white sharpness of her teeth. All of a sudden she feels cosy in mother's mouth, so cosy that she wouldn't want to leave it for anything in the world.

2

"What is your name?"
"Lejka."
"Lejka?"

4

"Lea Kralj," she corrected herself, raising her eyes from the beef broth that was pouring in a thin stream into a porcelain bowl. "At home they call me Lejka."

"Where's home?"

"Ljubljana."

"Ljubljana?"

"Do you know it?" She picked up the brass pot by the handle, some sort of samovar for bouillon, and waited for me to say yes. I admit that I had never heard of Ljubljana before, and that it was the first time in my life I had gone to the café in Madrid where she had suggested we meet, in which old locals sip beef broth all day.

I looked around as if I had suddenly thought of something, and went on with my questions. Her mother lived in Ljubljana, and so did she whenever she could, particularly in summer, always in summer, she said. She began to sing in Ljubljana, in a choir, and then left for Paris, where she did all sorts of odd jobs and studied with Madame Kudelka. Had I heard of Professor Kudelka? Lejka is thirty-seven. Not married, no children. She likes to go for walks, for hours. Orange is her favourite colour.

"Why are you asking me all this, Monsieur?"

She frowned and turned the samovar's spigot, stopping the flow of the bubbling yellowish stream into the bowl. She raised the bowl to her mouth and immediately, in that same instant, lowered it again. The broth was clearly too hot and had burned her lips.

"Because they say you came from nowhere."

"So, to you Ljubljana is nowhere?"

"What I'm trying to say is that nobody knows anything about you."

She lowered her face over the beef broth.

"Your career is practically blank, your repertoire unknown. You simply burst onto the scene. Yesterday, as a matter of fact."

She looked around.

"You must have read today's papers," I said, and began reciting the headlines: "A Prima Donna is Born – Triumph, then Flower-Flying Fury – The Heart and Soul of *Il Trittico* – New Prima Donna Spurns Roses."

"That's not true . . ."

"What's not true?"

"That I spurn roses."

"Well, what you did was hard to understand – but it was also unexpected, though I must say quite memorable."

"Is that why you wanted to interview me?"

"To some extent. A soprano who at the moment of her triumph flings a bouquet of red roses that one of the spectators has given her at the audience . . ."

She slammed down the bowl, the broth spattering over the counter. "Given? That bouquet came flying at me. It was a bouquet of red roses as you said, but with thorns!"

"The whole theatre was on its feet, wild with enthusiasm. And you . . ."

"These roses scratched my neck, my breasts, my arms . . . they stung me. What was I supposed to do?"

"You pressed them to you as if they were the most delicate flowers in the world. The audience went on shouting and stamping. It only fell silent when you walked to the

6

edge of the stage, untied the bouquet, and threw it with all your might, and then . . ."

"The bouquet came undone in the air all by itself . . ."

"All by itself? Perhaps . . . Not that I care," I suddenly said candidly, reaching for an empty bowl.

She leaned towards me as if she couldn't quite hear me.

"Then why are you asking me all this?" she whispered, suddenly wary.

"I wanted to see you up close," I whispered back.

She laughed abruptly, as if we had said everything, as if there were nothing more to be said. She folded back the sleeves of her raincoat and rested her elbows on the counter, as if to say: OK, here's my left profile, and here, if you like, you have me face on. Someone tried to squeeze between us at the counter, so I moved even closer to her. We looked straight at each other without embarrassment.

"So, that's that," she said, taking me by surprise, gathering up her things from the counter, and heading for the door.

"*Adiós*," she said, looking back, and then disappeared in the crowd.

3

Nobody had asked me to interview her. The editor of *Petronius* was on holiday, just as I was. I did it because of Pablo. Pablo was interested in everything, literature, opera, botany. I wanted to have something to tell him. But I can rephrase the question you're asking. For instance, what is the connection between Pablo Ortez and Lea Kralj? There is no connection. Except that if it had not been for Pablo, I would never have met Lea Kralj.

The following night I slept on his square futon. Pablo had a hard, sinewy body. Cords ran down his shoulders, gathered beneath his chest, frolicked down his sides, and stretched the length of his thighs and calves. Tightly twined cords covered with velvety skin. Whenever he let me spend the night with him in the back room of his Madrid flat, overlooking an inner courtyard overgrown with bamboo and a tree I didn't recognise, I always imagined he was made of scented, blond cords. *Loquerías, tonterías,* is what Pablo would have said if he had known what was flitting through my mind.

I sighed deeply and propped my head on my arms. In the room the night began to dissolve, the dark masses turning one by one into the *ficus benjamin,* the trembling aspen, and the sofa with his clothes . . . (mine were lying on the floor around the futon) . . . Piles of books from Divino . . . A dim lamp of milky opal . . . Flaking plaster on the ceiling . . . And his body next to mine. His back, still slightly tanned, though it was mid-October. His sides and bottom platonically pale in the early light. Between his thighs an infant's down that had sprouted into lusty hair. Hips firmly planted in the hard futon. Legs trustingly spread apart. Feet pointing downwards.

Eventually he rolled over on his side, as if he had heard what I was thinking. I moved over to the very edge of the futon and slipped a pillow under my head. That way I could see all of him. From head to foot. From his broad forehead, full eyebrows, high cheekbones and nonchalant lips, to his pale feet. Only his *ricardo* lay unconcerned between the top of his thighs and the linen sheet.

"Did you find out anything new?" he suddenly asked, feeling for the blanket without opening his eyes. The Madrid mornings had suddenly grown cooler. I leaned over him, covered him with the cotton bedcover that was lying on his side of the futon, and looked for my socks. I also felt a chill, but not because of the cold.

"Anything new," I echoed, and began putting on my socks. That was the last thing I expected him to say. No, Pablo, nothing new, I thought, staring at the spiral design in my socks. Nothing I had not been aware of from the start. In other words, that from time to time Pablo, out of the goodness of his heart, would open his bed to me, his hard, square futon that looks out on bamboo and the tree I don't recognise. That's just it, I repeated to myself: out of the goodness of his heart. Why should he not let me sleep or spend a sleepless night at his side? Why shouldn't he, after a long evening at the Divino bookshop, after our walking together through the wet town, after all the words we spoke, after all the *vino tinto* we drank, take off his flannel shirt, his stiff jeans, his weary socks, and his underpants – his underpants too – so that in the darkness I can finally imagine his tightly woven body, while he lies on his stomach and instantly sinks into the sleep of the innocent?

Pablo Ortez half rose on the futon, propping himself up on his elbows, and resting his head against the wall behind him. The cotton cover slipped down below his stomach, outlining his crossed legs. The sun timorously groped its

9

way over his powerful torso, his long neck, the perfect triangle of soft curly hair on his chest, the drapery of the cotton cover . . . I will say once and for all that he had the most attractive male body I have ever seen, and that I suddenly felt something very bitter in my mouth. I snatched up my glasses and my trousers, though I would have given anything not to have to put them on.

"About your prima donna," he said, his eyes still closed.

Now that's another matter, I thought with a long sigh, though the wound was already open. I walked across the room. The morning was still trying to force its way through the window. Madrid appeared on the wall in front of me – it had not been there a few moments ago. The first rays gently woke the noctambulant streets on the map of Pablo's birthplace. *Paseo de los melancólicos, Paseo de la esperanza* . . .

"What does she look like, up close?" he asked, suddenly wide-awake, only now opening his eyes.

I thought of her for the first time since the previous evening. I tried to visualise her again, as close up as I had seen her at the Coq Hardi when she stopped speaking and leaned her elbows on the counter.

"Tall. Not really beautiful, but not ugly either. It depends on the angle. Eyes that are grey and deeply etched. Grey, as if on the point of tears. Wearing a short raincoat, belted at the waist. And a scarf over her head, a bright scarf with colourful birds on a sandy background – all this on a warm October afternoon," I tallied up, finally pulling on my linen trousers. "And she's Slovenian. Have you ever come across a Slovenian before?"

He nodded. "Yes, I have." And then he asked, "Is that all?"

I tucked my undershirt into my trousers, and one by one did up the buttons of my fly.

4

No, it wasn't all. Lea Kralj and I had not met for the first time the day after the première of Puccini's *Il Trittico* at Madrid's Zarzuela in the downstairs area of the Coq Hardi, where one can stand at the counter and have a quick beef broth and triangular meat pies. In a sense, we had met backstage at the Zarzuela a few days before the premiere. Pablo was an old acquaintance of Señor Joaquino, one of the two directors of the Zarzuela, a loyal customer of the Divino bookshop and a reincarnation of Valle-Inclán (a robust beard and head of hair, and an empty sleeve, Pablo had told me) – anyway, Señor Joaquino was someone who could give me permission to watch the final rehearsals of *Il Trittico*. I had to find a way to keep busy in Madrid. Pablo spent his days in the Divino and his nights on the hard futon in the back room with the view of the bamboo and the tall tree. I knew no-one but him, some passing clients of his, and Cecilia, a photographer.

One long Madrid afternoon, the week before the premiere (only in Ljubljana can afternoons without a siesta be longer than those in Madrid), I went to the doorman of the Teatro de la Zarzuela and asked to see Señor Joaquino. The doorman waved me through, telling me to look for him in the orchestra, on the first balcony, on stage, backstage, or wherever else he might be. So I set out to track down Valle-Inclán, as Pablo, with his knack for physiognomies and his grasp of Spanish literature, had called him. I pushed open the two doors, whose heavy swing propelled me into the hall. On stage there was hammering, scenery was being moved, spotlights were being mounted. In the orchestra there were a few heads, but none that bore any resemblance to Valle-Inclán. The first balcony was empty. The loges, from what I could see from the balcony, were empty too. The lighting director was firmly planted on the stage, shouting orders in French: *Beaucoup de lumière à la cour, Messieurs! Je veux qu'on voie les visages ... Les visages ...*

Before long, I got lost backstage. The projection room, the first corridor, the second, costumes, all kinds of props, artificial flowers, artificial flowers everywhere, wild artificial flowers, who would have thought ... Among them rosemary and thyme, if I'm not mistaken, and behind a long clothes rack with a medley of trousers and starched shirts, I suddenly saw a woman's eyes. For a while, I could only see her eyes staring at me as if they did not see me. Then the whole scene came into view: a woman in a theatrical costume with a long red and green skirt, her arms around a man in a black T-shirt of the kind worn by stagehands. She was standing, in a way, leaning against the wall. The man was plunging into her with deep thrusts in an unusual rhythm. He stopped with each thrust, clinging to her and then again driving into her with all his might. Her eyes dimmed with every thrust, collapsed, sank into themselves ... and then again gazed at me, at least that is what I thought. Astonished, ready, waiting for the coup de grâce . . . Go for it! I urged the man's back, despite myself. Go for it! . . . Suddenly, as if he had heard me, he threw her onto a nearby table, brusquely and vehemently, her red and green dress flying over her face. She rasped from underneath, as if she had laughed out loud. Again he drove into her, powerfully and just once, the table moaning beneath them. I stood behind the medley of trousers and starched shirts without moving, unable to look away. *Je veux qu'on voie les visages . . . Les visages . . .* I heard again from a distance.

Obviously I could not have known at that time that Lea Kralj had many ancillary affairs. Ancillary, *ancilla* as in maidservant, inferior . . . Affairs that were quick, hidden, backstage . . . With men she happened to come across and who were in every way beneath her, in other words, socially and intellectually. Stagehands, electricians, hair and make-up artists . . . but preferably, God knows why, stagehands. Nor did I know that her name was Lea Kralj and that a week later I would see her as the great, sinful Angelica, who after a triumphant premiere, in the midst of thunderous applause, walks to the edge of the orchestra pit, and with all her might hurls into the auditorium the bouquet of dark red roses that a few moments earlier had come flying at her. I was seeking Valle-Inclán and had stumbled upon Angelica. And when I phoned her for an interview and she appeared in the downstairs area of the Coq Hardi the following day, raising her dark glasses, I saw the same grey eyes that had gazed at me before they were covered by the bright skirt.

I don't know whether she recognised me. We never spoke

of it later either, as if the scene backstage at the Zarzuela were not part of our story. But when we stood in silence next to each other for a few moments at the counter of the Coq Hardi, I suddenly had the impression that she did know that our eyes had met before. And when she was leaving and called out "*Adiós*", I told myself that her *adiós* really meant goodbye, that her sex life had absolutely nothing to do with me, that our ways would now part, and that we would not meet again so soon – or ever – and that she would continue singing Angelica, Jenufa, Katya, Violetta . . . that she would make love to stagehands, perhaps again hurl thorny roses at the audience. And as for me . . . she knew nothing about me other than my being a chance voyeur and some sort of journalist. To each his own, so *adiós, adiós.*

5

Pablo loved watermelons, gazpacho, green salad, *calamares con la tinta*. Bitter coffee, goat cheese, tapas from the Plaza Mayor. Things he had heard strangers say, particularly: "Tomorrow I will be righteous and bold, but not today." Blossoming chestnut trees. Going for walks beneath blossoming chestnut trees . . . Checked flannel shirts – pale, washed-out checks . . . Stiff jeans and well-worn shoes, well-worn, laced, brown Salamander shoes, size 10½ . . . Short hair, rough, unshaven cheeks. The most beautiful woman was Ava Smith Field, alias Ava Gardner, he said, but so were Marta, Cecilia, Nieves, Ana-María, Blanca, Carmen,

Sybil, Milena, Fanny, Mimi, and the beguiling Señora García Fernández, one of his best clients. Lying in late in the morning on his hard futon, from time to time even with me, though strictly platonically . . . Plants, all plants. Long, concentrated study, or persistent daily self-improvement. The street he was born on, the Calle María de Molina, where his father, Joaquin Pasqual Ortez, a retired geographer, was living out his life. The Calle Divino Pastor. His bookshop, Divino, a most selective store, ladies and gentlemen, novelesque, the novel as the entrance to life, but through the narrow doorway of Pablo Ortez, Pablo Ortez only sells the books of his personal Pantheon. When you step into the narrow Divino bookshop from the street called Divino Pastor that inspired its name, you step into the imaginary garden of Pablo Ortez: to the right, in the place of honour, are *Anna Karenina*, *The Brothers Karamazov*, but also *The Princess of Cleves*, *The Charterhouse of Parma*, *Lost Illusions*, and *Lady Chatterley's Lover*; to the left, no less visible, compatriots like Javier Marías, Antonio Muñoz Molina, and even Juan Manuel de Prada . . . across from Philip Roth, of course. *Vino tinto*, exclusively *tinto*. Just as exclusively, Cameron de la Isla. Taking his time. "It is time that is in a hurry, not me," he liked to say. Wednesdays, when the beguiling Señora García Fernández came in through the back door. Friday evenings, because Ana-María was free. Mondays, because Sunday was over. The botanical gardens in the Parque del Retiro, particularly the left-hand section with its poisonous shrubs, *daphne mezereum, daphne creorum, daphne laureola, atropa belladonna* . . . the row of tall silver maples. The tall silver maples. Long walks through town . . . Words like venerate, sob, shoreline, clatter, cower, plane tree, single file . . . Pablo loved all this and much more . . . Except me. Me he did not love.

6

"'Señorita, my blood-group is B-positive,' you whispered to me. I happened to be passing. I was roaming the streets after my performance at the Zarzuela. I was lost . . . This is my first time singing in Madrid . . . I was looking for a taxi. A few paces away from a bar called Marin . . . Mario . . . I can't remember the name . . . or the street . . . but that hardly matters. It was around two o'clock, half past two at night, or rather, in the morning. You were lying on the pavement, no, in the street with your head on the pavement . . . I didn't recognise you right away . . . I crouched down next to you. I raised your head, your shoulders . . . I thought you were lying in a pool of blood. But you weren't bleeding, not a drop or a hint of a drop . . . Though you kept repeating: 'Señorita, my blood-group is B-positive.' You were pale, pale as a . . . as a wall, as a sheet . . . But entirely calm. I went to call a doctor. I was worried the bleeding might be internal. The bar was teeming with people. A young man with green hair was breathing into the telephone by the toilets. He cocked his middle finger at me, *hija de puta* . . . So I told myself that everything must be all right, since you weren't bleeding. I sat down next to you, on the pavement. I told myself that somebody might come looking for you. Perhaps you were waiting for someone. But people just walked by. Someone even stepped over you . . . A tall man with a bunch of keys jingling on his belt . . . The bar on the corner began to empty out . . . The air was growing increasingly chilly. At least, I began to feel cold. I stopped the first taxi I saw. I asked the driver to help me. I had to promise that you wouldn't vomit in the taxi, that I knew you. Otherwise he wouldn't have taken us. 'I don't take people who vomit in my taxi, Señorita,' he said to me. We lifted you onto the back seat. I told him you had Raynaud's illness, no, Raynaud's Syndrome, which reassured him. The name of an illness always has a reassuring effect . . . Even though you did reek of alcohol and were all crumpled up, whiter than a shroud, in short, you could easily have vomited. But most fortunately, you didn't. I don't want to have to clean out the car, Señorita, he told me, you know what I mean. I know, I know. We carried you up to my hotel room. Just try picturing that . . . We laid you on the bed. Antonio even took off your shoes. His name was Antonio. Because after that he sat down next to you on the bed and wanted to chat. I poured the two of us a glass of whisky. What was I doing with you in Madrid? I wasn't with you. Then did I even know you? Barely. Then what were you doing in my room? Good question, a very good question. Then what was I doing in Madrid? Singing. What, singing? Yes, singing. And where did I sing? The Zarzuela. The Zarzuela? He'd never heard of it . . . Finally he left. I undressed and lay down beside you . . . You didn't move all night . . . You were like a dead man . . . You slept like a corpse."

17

7

It wasn't at all clear to me, either. Our beginning was precisely like that: incoherent, incomprehensible, indecipherable.

"Tell me once more what happened," I said to her, though the last thing I wanted to do was to reconstruct that night on which she found me lying in the street. Everything I was doing those days, and particularly that night, had precisely the opposite aim: to forget, to escape, static on the screen, off the air, not-I, not-Madrid, tomorrow I will be righteous and bold, but not today . . . I only wanted to reconstruct a single moment, the one in which her face leaned down over me. To place it in the chain of our encounters: the Zarzuela, the Coq Hardi, Bar Marienbad . . . But what was she doing in the Calle de la Cabeza? At two or three in the morning, not far from the Marienbad . . . How had she just happened to find me there? She of all people? Just at the moment when my cocktail of sleeping pills and alcohol imploded. When I began to slip slowly out of myself, when I had walked a few steps from the door of the Marienbad, and then a few more, when I had bumped into someone, who knows, a man or a woman, who punched me in the stomach; when I had grabbed hold of something solid, something hard and metallic, when the night became impenetrably thick with fluorescent stars above me, when the cold metallic object eluded me, when I tried to grab hold of it again, to grab hold of it at all costs; but it did not want me, no-one wanted me; when I looked helplessly into the darkness above me . . . How was it that her face with its headscarf leaned over me as if it wanted to cover me with a blanket at that precise moment, on the edge of consciousness?

At that moment, of course, I did not know that the face was hers. I somehow reconstructed the story the following morning. Why am I in this hotel room, in this unmade double bed? Who slept next to me? Whose women's clothes are scattered about the room? The bottle of whisky on the table. Who is taking a shower in the bathroom? Why do I have a sharp pain at the back of my neck?

I reconstructed her when she sat at the head of the bed. Lea Kralj in a white, hotel dressing-gown. Her hair still wet, hanging loose over her nape, a few drops trickling down her temples and neck, which she wiped away with her sleeve. Her neck was long and her complexion very light, with a few yellowish freckles beneath the eyes. She was holding a glass of water and two aspirin. While they dissolved in a fizz, she told me how she had found me lying on the pavement the night before and had brought me to her hotel in a taxi.

"Strange, don't you think? I've only been in Madrid for three weeks, it'll be three weeks tomorrow . . . And in those three weeks we've seen each other . . . twice," she said, putting the glass down on the bedside table. "Drop the key off at the desk when you leave," she added.

I tried to nod and shake my head at the same time. To nod that I would drop the key off at the desk, and to shake my head because we had met three times, even four, if you counted the première of Puccini's *Il Trittico*. A sharp pain shot through my head, and I had to close my eyes.

I heard her moving about the room. Pouring herself coffee, drinking in long sips . . . Going into the bathroom. Turning on the tap . . . Vocalising, yes, vocalising . . . While the water was pouring loudly into the tub . . . Selecting clothes from the wardrobe . . . From two wardrobes . . . Rummaging in drawers, opening a new packet of tights, sitting down in the armchair, putting them on . . . Carefully throwing the wrapper into the rubbish. From time to time I opened my eyes. Where were my glasses? Her legs looked awkward. Or rather, uneven. There was a certain uneven-ness about her. Her legs and arms were too long. Her hair, light brown, ash blond, even straw blond, depending on the light, was now dry, and hung to her shoulders. She sat down at the table in front of the mirror and lit a cigarette. I didn't know that opera singers could smoke. She passed the cigarette a couple of times from one hand to the other while she was writing something. She was wearing a short green dress with three-quarter sleeves that at first glance was a little out of fashion. Wearing the same summer shoes I had seen her in at the Coq Hardi. No, her dress was not out of fashion. Maybe just a bit too big. Perhaps she should draw her hair back, to show off her décolleté. Hmm, I watched her in the mirror, she should draw her hair back. She went into the other room. The phone rang. She came back wearing a raincoat. Is it raining? She was wearing her headscarf with the colourful birds.

"Hello, hello . . . *dígame*," she said.

She sat down by the table with the phone, not far from

the mirror. I could see her face. Suddenly she began talking in another language. Slovene, I said to myself, since she's Slovenian. She answered tersely, from time to time uttering a long sentence . . . Her voice had changed when she started speaking her own language. Different from French, which she spoke with me. In a different register, deeper, more cerebral. Then something must have happened. All of a sudden she seemed lost. With one hand she fumbled nervously with the hem of her scarf. Several times she sighed deeply. When she hung up, I saw her eyes instantly fill with tears. She angrily wiped them away with her headscarf and bit her lower lip. Then she walked over to the mirror and looked at herself. She dried her eyes again and tied the scarf over her head. Without even saying goodbye – I think she had forgotten about me – she turned and left the room.

8

It is hard to say what impression she left on me. An opera singer, a Slovenian, whom I met a few times in succession in Madrid. A woman in whose bed I lay, who dressed in front of me, drank coffee, tidied up, telephoned, vocalised in the bathroom, lit a cigarette . . . I studied her the way I studied the pattern of the bedcover, the lamp by the television, the reproduction of *Santa Casilda* on the wall in front of me, the writing utensils, her black jacket, or her headscarf. Later, when people began to call her "The prima donna who knows how to die", "The Slovenian", or simply "La Kralj", I often tried to imagine that young man – me, who spent two and a half days in the hotel room of an unknown woman – her. But at that point I wasn't asking myself those kinds of questions. Quite the contrary. I was trying once again to empty my head, static on the screen, off the air . . . And above all, to remain in her hotel room as long as possible, by whatever means.

"Again? Do I have to tell you everything all over again?" she said, as if she were imitating me, the same Parisian accent, the same insincere look. A red flush spread over her cheeks.

"Yes," I said with a nod.

"Where do you want me to start? From 'My blood-group is B-positive,' or from the first morning in this room, when the fine young gentleman chose to wake up and open his eyes? Or perhaps from this morning, when his appetite returned and he ate two breakfasts, his and mine?" she said, her voice rising.

"As you wish," I replied, hoping to calm her.

"As I wish? Well, thank you! Thank you very much! For two days I've been telling you the same story. In great detail. How I found you half-conscious in the street. How people just walked by. How I stopped a taxi. And so on . . . In the hope that you would remember something . . . Your name, if nothing else!"

She turned around, walked a few steps, took hold of the armchair, pulled it towards the bed, and sat down. She crossed her arms and legs and looked at me. It was the first time I saw her wearing make-up. Her face was sterner, more serious, more even. There was a short, fine crease on each cheek.

"And now you want me to start over again from the beginning . . . So listen carefully, my accidental friend, as I will tell the story one . . . last . . . time." She drew out the final phrase.

She pulled her armchair closer and crossed her legs in the opposite direction.

"I am also watching you, you know. It's not just you who's watching me," she began. "From the time you woke up after that night of yours. From that point on I haven't believed in your . . . your amnesia. Amnesia, indeed! Ever since, I've been wondering what it is you're doing in my room . . . in my bed! What the hell are you up to? The time has come for you to answer me. Face to face, the way we were at the Coq Hardi . . . This evening is my last performance. I'm leaving tomorrow."

"Tomorrow?"

"Tomorrow," she repeated.

We looked at each other for a few moments. I tried to think of something to say. Then I pulled back the covers and went to get my clothes that lay folded on the chair near the bathroom. I put on my trousers and the sweat-shirt that still bore the traces of my first and only night of real amnesia. I looked at myself for an instant in the mirror above the writing table. I was no longer white as a shroud. But that didn't mean I had to leave her room that very moment. I went over to the minibar and took out the bottle of whisky. I felt her eyes following me: what the hell does this man think he's doing . . . Really! . . . In those two days I had had the opportunity to study every single one of her daily habits: her first morning coffee, breakfast, her long ablutions, the vocalisation in the bathroom . . . Tidying up the room, piling up bed linen, jackets, scores, magazines, all with incredible fervour, everything where it belonged, face creams, make-up, perfume in the bathroom, the tights in the drawer. Her second morning coffee, which she ordered over the phone . . . And then in the late afternoon, around six, half past six, when the sun began to sink behind the Puerta del Sol, when the sky was covered with a dark, unsettling gauze, a glass of whisky.

I poured two glasses.

"I'll tell you everything," I said, suddenly capitulating. "But you also have to promise to answer a question. No, two questions."

She picked up her glass and drank a sip.

"Who'll go first?" she asked, yielding despite herself.

"Me."

We both made ourselves comfortable, she leaning back in her armchair, I leaning against the wall behind the bed. She took off her shoes, pulled in one leg beneath the other, and rested her chin on her palm. She had long, delicate hands, without rings, without anything, hands that work, I thought. And innocent, if hands can be innocent. She was again somehow peculiarly dressed: a short skirt, drawn in at the waist, with a pattern of large flowers, a light blue jacket with only the top buttons fastened, and rolled-up sleeves. Low-heeled shoes, also light blue, were placed neatly together in front of the armchair. Suddenly she was no longer in such a hurry. And suddenly she really started to interest me.

"What is Raynaud's Syndrome?" I asked her.

24

"There we go! I knew your memory was beginning to come back. It is a very rare disease, in which under the effect of intense cold or emotional shock, the flow of blood to the fingers and toes is interrupted. Your extremities turn yellow and hurt quite a lot, especially when the blood returns to the veins. No danger. Just one of those many little inexplicable conditions . . . What was the other question?"

"Who called you yesterday on the phone?"

"Yesterday?"

"When you were crying."

She turned her head to the side, as if to think.

"My mother," she finally replied.

9

Then it was my turn. I don't know if this is of any interest to you. Let's say it is. My futile love for Pablo. Our life together in Madrid. "Together" is obviously not the right word, nor was life in Madrid really "ours". I should say two weeks, two and a half weeks a year. For the last three years. Usually in autumn. Autumn in Madrid, in Pablo Ortez's flat. The gradual yellowing of the trees in the Parque del Retiro. The maples, the wild cherry trees, *taxus baccata*, *aconitum vulparia*, and other poisonous shrubs in the botanical garden. The diseased plane trees of the Arganzuela. And Divino, with Cervantes, Rabelais, Madame de Sévigné, artillery officer Laclos, but also many obscure authors whom Pablo displayed prominently . . . Pablo's introducing me to literature, botany, and unrequited love. Love without recompense, gratis, basically because he is he and I am me. Because early one afternoon three years ago, he had sat down at my table, rolled up the sleeves of his checked shirt, leaned his strong, curly-haired forearms on the table, ordered a glass of *vino tinto*, opened a book, and begun to read. Because he read late into the afternoon and part of the evening, because he did not let himself be disturbed, because he did not blink at all, because he sat there as if he were rooted to the spot. Because he moved his lips only now and then, as if he were silently repeating a word or a sentence from the book. Because he also let me read, because he was like an open book, Pablo Ortez, thirty-nine, at first glance an anarchist, or perhaps a man with leftist tendencies, a francophone, atheist, heterosexual man from Madrid. Because he had an intense forehead, full eyebrows, the white of his eyes clear, a soft feminine mouth, and a tightly twined body. Because he was leaning back in his chair as if he were at the beach, offering his body to the sun. Because he had raised his eyes and looked at me when he closed the book. Because he seemed surprised, as if we had seen each other somewhere before, ah, of course – he ran his hand though his short hair – of course we had, at the beginning of his book. Because he had ordered two more glasses of *vino tinto*, because he had spoken first. Because he had pulled his chair closer, like you just did right now, because he was again surprised: what was I doing in Madrid in this miserable café, *o dios*? And because I suddenly knew what I was doing there. Because I pressed my lips tight the way I was to do later, every time the words congealed in my throat. Because I had smiled and immersed myself in the calm waters of his eyes. That incomparable love. Truly incomparable. Somewhat later – and only once – I kissed him on the lips. I don't know what came over me, I really don't. We were standing in the Divino, among the books. The evening sun licked their spines and our shoulders. All of a sudden I wanted to taste the flavour of his mouth. I leaned towards him, without thinking. My body was faster than my mind. Pablo grabbed me hard by the shoulders and pushed me away, against the bookshelves. What got into your head! he exclaimed. Luckily, the shop bell rang and we heard steps. A new reader. So we weren't even obliged to look at one another. Yes, really, what had got into my head? You have, I could have told him. You have taken root in me . . . Day and night you are lurking inside me. At any moment you can see yourself in me. My inner shadow, my sharp pain . . . From time to time I try to still it . . . Like that night with the cocktail of sleeping pills and alcohol. If I were dirt in the gutter, I would let myself be washed away . . . Like Antonio Banderas in *Tie Me Up, Tie Me Down* . . . But the anaesthesia was short-lived, unfortunately transient . . . I tried to prolong it . . . So that I would only have the face of the prima donna before me . . . Do you understand?

10

Even now, as I try to answer your question about how we first met as precisely as possible, and am looking for a more logical course of events, I cannot find one. One thing is certain: there was no connection between Pablo and her hotel room. And when I opened my eyes in her bed and saw before me a woman in a white towelling dressing-gown, it was her. She was holding a glass of water with effervescing aspirin, and started telling me the story: Señorita, my blood-group is B-positive . . . and so on. And as I was listening to her, my head splitting with pain, I suddenly remembered her face and her headscarf leaning down towards me like a dark icon. It had the face of the Slovenian prima donna whom I had seen for the first time backstage at the Zarzuela. And without seeing that face I most probably would never have left Madrid early or said goodbye for ever to Pablo.

The same day, I suggested to Pablo that we go for a walk in our park. I counted the steps, I remember it as if it were yesterday. Still 5000, 4800, 4751 . . . I went through compli-cated mental calculations because I did not want our final steps together to end in sadness. Even at the word "final" I felt a shudder run through me: my final afternoon in Madrid, my final walk with Pablo, the final performance of *Suor Angelica* with the Slovenian prima donna in the leading role, her final night in the hotel room that I had come to know to its minutest detail . . . Pablo was not aware that we were about 3000 steps away from the botanical garden, and that these would probably be our last steps together. He was walking next to me without sensing that anything was amiss. He asked me where I had been the last few days, where I had slept, why I hadn't dropped by at the Divino, why I hadn't knocked on the door of his room . . . He looked at me with that hard whiteness in his eyes, from time to time moistening his lips with his tongue. One hand, the hand next to me, was swinging regularly back and forth, in the other he was holding a copy of *El País*. The top two buttons of his blue checked shirt were open over his chest, his face an extension of the damp triangle of the skin. Another 3150 steps . . . And if we don't enter through the main gate, another 100, 110 to the side entrance near the big Lebanese cedar. Which means altogether 3140 . . . 3030 . . . Had I sent in my interview, he wanted to know. Had I heard anything new about the Slovenian prima donna? One of his clients, a bookkeeper at the local gasworks, an old opera buff, had told him about her . . . I answered with a yes and a no, while I counted our steps and wondered if there was another side entrance beyond the one near the Lebanese cedar. For a moment I thought of telling him everything. In those 2800 steps that separated us from the side entrance of the botanical garden. That I would leave Madrid early because of him and her . . . Because of him and her? Because of him and her: without him I would not have come to Madrid. As far as I was concerned, Madrid might just as well have been called Pablo Ortez. My Madrid turned around a single axis. All its streets poured into a single intersection. Without him, without that inner shadow . . . he knows exactly what I am talking about, we both know what it's about, so, without that inner shadow, that trenchant pain, I would never have seen her face above me . . . The face at the entrance of a tunnel, at the extreme edge of consciousness, the face that leaned over me as if it wanted to cover me with a blanket . . . Without him I would never have woken up in her bed . . . She would not have sat down next to me in her towelling dressing-gown with

29

wet hair . . . She would not have brought me a glass of water with aspirin . . . Dressed a few metres away from me . . . Or vocalised in the bathroom . . . Just as she would not have slept next to me. When did I last sleep next to a woman? . . . And the following day, after a long afternoon, we would not have sat facing one another, each with a glass of whisky. Somehow pleasant, cosy, as if we had just come home and taken off our shoes . . . Another 800, 750 steps together . . . No, much less . . . From a distance I saw the main entrance to the botanical garden. Three hundred paces at most . . . Where was I? Without him, without the attraction I felt for him, I would never have exchanged confidences with the Slovenian prima donna in room seventeen on the first floor of the Hotel Escorial. My mother, she said. I kissed him only once, I wanted to know the taste of his mouth, I told her. Without him she would not have taken me to the door of her hotel room and said: I think that's that. How simple . . . I think that's that. Is it possible to say it any better? I think that's that. I think that's that, Pablo. A farewell beneath the silver maples, not far from the poisonous shrubs, *daphne mezereum, daphne creorum, daphne laureola, atropa belladonna* . . . But without any theatricality, as I promised myself. Seventeen, seventeen, seventeen . . . I stopped. Is something wrong? Pablo asked me. No, no, I shook my head, why should there be . . . Thirteen, twelve . . . No other side entrance . . . Just the central exit . . . The exit is always central . . . Our last steps . . . The maples look at us from a distance . . . One last time.

I I

If I could do it again. That's my weakness, my leitmotiv, my mania, the question I ask myself. From time to time with outright self-satisfaction. If I could do it again, I tell myself, if I were to find myself in the same circumstances, I would do exactly the same thing. But mostly out of sheer weakness, even desperation. If I could do it again, I tell myself, groping for that point where everything fell apart and where I would still have been able to take that other path. If I had another chance with Pablo I would, I think, let matters run their course until our meeting by the pillar of that miserable café that smelled of deep-fried oil. I definitely would want to see him walking once more towards my table, rolling up the sleeves of his checked shirt, leaning his strong, curly-haired forearms on the table, ordering a glass of *vino tinto*, opening a book, and beginning to read. I would let him read late into the afternoon and part of the evening, not letting him out of my sight for an instant. I would gaze at his broad forehead, his feminine mouth, his smooth neck, the two open buttons of his shirt, the one hand on his knee . . . Perhaps I would even wait for him to close the book and raise his eyes and look at me, to seem surprised, as if we had seen each other somewhere before: of course – he ran his hand through his hair – at the beginning of the book. I would even wait for him to order two more glasses of *vino tinto*, to pull his chair closer, and begin to talk. Yes, I would let him talk, let his eyes light up, or rather that blue-white colour in them . . . And then, in the middle of the most pleasant conversation in the world, about his little bookshop Divino, about *Petronius*, about plants, all sorts of plants, about Madrid's noctambulant streets, I would suddenly get up, yes, get up, shake hands, feel his touch for the first and last time, feel his palm in mine, and then *adiós*, Pablo, *adiós*. The door would fall shut behind me. I would never have returned to Madrid, never set foot in the Calle Divino Pastor, in the Divino bookshop, never spent the night on the hard futon in the back room of his Madrid flat overlooking an inner courtyard overgrown with bamboo and a tree I did not recognise. I never would have spent the evening and part of the night at the bar in the Calle de la Cabeza, not to mention the implosive cocktail of sleeping pills and alcohol. And, I suddenly realise, I would never have met the Slovenian prima donna. Of course not. How could she have found me on the pavement if I wasn't there, or rather if I had not wanted to slip out of myself. No, stop, back to the café. What were you saying, Pablo?

If I could do it again, I would want to meet the Slovenian prima donna again.

12

It was not in Madrid that I became her companion, as you put it, but in Paris. I know that she used the word companion too. With time, I got used to it. Of course, companion, why not? What else could she have called me? Her watcher, admirer, *cicisbeo*? Or even betrayer? When I returned to Paris after Madrid – Paris was my city, as Ljubljana was hers – she disappeared from my life for a while. "Who's that?" friends asked whenever I happened to mention her name, so that at times it seemed to me I had only dreamt of the roses, the effervescing aspirin, the towelling hotel dressing-gown. I often came across her name in magazines, especially music publications. "Amazing Slovenian soprano", "The new face of opera", "With her, opera is no longer stagnating, and Brahms no longer a composer for neurotics". No, it had not been a dream. A few months later I read the following: "After Madrid and Amsterdam, prima donna finally arrives in Paris".

It was in the early spring of 1997, I still remember her arrival. It was the arrival of spring. That was exactly the feeling I had: that spring had come to me, that it was in the middle of the morning that the sun appeared from behind the neighbouring house, slithered over to my bed, nudged my shoulder, opened my eyes, and gazed at itself in them. Good morning, it whispered to me, you who are only now waking to a new day. I passed my hand over my face. It's true, I replied, blinking. I, who only now am waking to a new day. My palm smelled of genitals. Whose, I wondered, and sniffed at my hand intently. The tall, elegant geo-politician from the Caucasus, or Lieutenant-Colonel Haas, alias the Little Prince? I went over to the window and opened it wide. Come in, I told the Spring. As I opened the second and third window, I only gave it a nod. Below me, the street and the hospital across the way were teeming with life. A chestnut tree, under which a few children were standing, was blossoming in the garden in front of the hospital. I picked up my jacket from the floor by the window and wrapped it around me. Come in, Spring, even if you are still cool, even chilly, in the mid-morning. I poured myself a glass of milk, took a long sip, and stood in front of the mirror that was leaning against the wall. I sat down in front of it with my glass of milk, and looked at the room in the mirror.

Despite everything, this is still my home, I thought. This large, long and narrow room into which spring had just entered, is my home, because apart from the cries of the new-born infants, I don't have to listen to anyone. I can leave my grey jacket lying on the floor, my trousers, socks, the few books I have, CDs, bottles of alcohol, magazines . . . my green glass vase with the dark orange amaryllises. And my rubbish. It's very important for a feeling of home to have one's rubbish. And the large mirror in front of which I was sitting and in which I was gazing at my glass of milk, my home, and myself. You spend too much time looking at yourself in the mirror, my Aunt Anna had warned me. Even Lieutenant-Colonel Haas had asked me: Why do you like gazing at your reflection so much?

Early that spring Lea Kralj settled in Paris too. I knew everything: The fifth floor of the Hôtel Régent, room 57, about twenty, twenty-five minutes away from my place by bicycle, or a few *métro* stations and one transfer. She was to appear in the role of Katya Kabanova in Leoš Janáček's opera, under the baton of the famous Sir Charles Mackerras and the direction of the Catalan director Lluis Toronto, who had also staged *Il Trittico* at the Zarzuela. But that early spring, Aunt Anna and Lieutenant-Colonel Haas, I was not gazing at my reversed image. In that big mirror, which even now is leaning against the wall of my room, I tried to see the man who in a few days would be standing before the woman he had met in Madrid the previous autumn. "Met" is not the word. Collided. Stopped in front of her. As she later also collided with me. Stopped in front of me. Leaned down over me, as if she wanted to cover me with a blanket. Perhaps she even saved my life. In my mirror I wanted to see myself in advance through her eyes, to be astonished in her name: Well, well! Who would have thought! My young amnesiac friend from the hotel in Madrid ... To prepare myself for her, to familiarise myself with the terrain, as my alter ego Lieutenant-Colonel Haas would say.

13

"Are you sure you know her?" the receptionist of the Hôtel Régent asked, somewhat taken aback, rolling her chair forwards so she could look me in the eye. She rested her chin on her palm: "Do you at least know what she looks like?"

That's a good question. I stared back at her. A pale creature with nimble fingers, which she drummed on the counter. Then she picked up the phone and gave a short laugh. Had she not picked up the phone at that moment and laughed, I would have tried to explain. Our consecutive encounters in Madrid, the morning she had sat down next to me with the effervescing aspirin, when she had dressed so I could see her black frilly undergarments, tele-phoned, drank coffee, the two nights we slept next to each other . . . Does that mean we know each other?

"She'll be down in ten minutes. I've called a taxi for her," the receptionist said, covering the receiver with her hand.

I installed myself on a sofa behind a Greek column. I wanted to surprise her, the prima donna. I wanted to walk up to her, see the surprise spreading over her face, hear her soft, hoarse voice or even her short laugh, as at the Coq Hardi. I watched the hotel guests coming and going between the two Greek columns, mainly heterosexual couples, dressed to the nines, made up and perfumed, on their way out to dinner. So much bad taste in a few square metres, I thought. One couple – a tall, corpulent man with glasses accompanied by a thin blonde in a semi-transparent dress – fell apart, one could say, before my very eyes. When they had almost left my field of vision, the blonde suddenly lost her balance, staggered, and cried out. In an instant she became half a head shorter. She looked reluctantly at her foot, and then even more reluctantly around her.

"Your heel broke off," the man with the glasses said, as if he had just made a great discovery.

The blonde glanced at him coldly and limped over to the nearest armchair. She took off her vertiginous shoe, placed it on her lap, and gazed at it forlornly. The corpu-lent bespectacled man shuffled over to her chair and sighed deeply. At that moment I heard a familiar voice. It came precisely from behind the corpulent back. I got up and walked past him. I leaned against the Greek column. How was it that I had heard her voice, I asked myself. Then I

36

saw her. If she had not been wearing her headscarf I might not have recognised her. So that's her, I said to myself. That woman in the tight, short skirt, black jacket with only the top buttons fastened, and tennis shoes (were my eyes deceiving me?), who is holding some sort of folder or package and is coming towards me with long, resolute steps. That woman with the thin face, who despite her sunglasses could just as well be a pharmacist or the pale and drawn wife of a busy director of the timber industry in a central European country on a business trip to Paris.

I stood leaning against the column and waited. I felt my face preparing for the expression of domesticity that I had seen in my mirror. By the time I had stepped away from the column, swallowed hard, and reached out my hand, she had walked past me. She stopped in front of the receptionist, put her package down on the counter, and began telling her something. From time to time she turned and looked towards the entrance. From behind, she seemed older than she really was. I saw that her hair, peering out from under her headscarf, had grown longer. She asked for some paper and a pencil and began to write.

I walked over to her. All of a sudden, as if she and I had stood only a pace away from each other, I was standing next to her. I smelled her perfume. I could easily have reached out and touched her shoulder. I saw her hand hurrying over the paper. The receptionist looked at me in surprise and nodded at me, that this was her and that I should say something. What was I waiting for?

"My blood-group is still B-positive," I heard my voice say. "What about yours?"

Only then did she turn towards me.

She took off her glasses and looked at me. The surface of her eyes moved as if something had flown against them. Her eyes are really the colour of tears, it flashed through my mind. Light grey, almost transparent, as if she had a cold. And beneath them and near her nose she still had the yellowish freckles. She suddenly bit her lower lip the way she had done in the hotel room in Madrid when she was angry at me. Only now she was not angry at me, at least that's how it seemed to me. But she did not seem pleased either.

"My what?" she asked.

"Your taxi," came a voice from outside the door, where a man in livery was standing.

"Ah yes, my taxi," she murmured, still biting her lip. I nodded. I should have known. After all, the receptionist had told me that she had called a taxi for her.

"I'm not going anywhere with you," a voice behind my back shrieked. The thin blonde had got up from the armchair and was walking barefoot to the lift.

When I looked back towards the door, Lea Kralj was already in the taxi, and leaning her head forwards to the driver.

14

God knows I don't have much to say about myself and everything that happened during that spring in Paris. I am relying on Lea Kralj, who was my best mirror. If it is true that there is something botanical in every person's physiognomy, then I was at first glance a plant that was discreet, fairly inconspicuous, and banal, but also delicate and quite decorative, a plant that one only noticed if one was standing right next to it and taking the trouble to examine it for a while. I was twenty-seven (exactly ten years younger than Lea Kralj), and nothing much had happened to me beyond my parents' accidental death when I was a child, the death of Aunt Anna when I was a young man, the many moves and just as many studies that I started but never finished, a few minor affairs, my inappropriate love for Pablo. When I say that I am not a particularly interesting person, I'm not being coy or falsely modest. I wouldn't put it this way today. Now I would say that I didn't see further than two metres in front of me, and that therefore I could not see beyond myself.

When I wasn't scribbling for the magazine *Petronius Arbiter* (where I was responsible for the penultimate page, "Against the Grain", in which I published among other things my first and only interview with Lea Kralj, "Close-up", a few news items about her, and a very short piece on Slovenia), I went to the cinema, rode my bicycle through Paris, which I know like the back of my hand, or paced up and down my long and narrow room. I delighted in the spring, which here and there surged up in me, dazzled me, exchanged glances with me. Good morning, even though it is already almost noon, spring said to me with a touch of austerity. I ran my hand over my face. My sex life was average, not more, not less. I jumped up. With a glass of milk between my feet I sat down in front of the mirror, which was standing on the floor like everything else at my place. For a long time I looked into it, preparing my face for the Slovenian prima donna.

One day she and I finally will stop in front of one another, I thought. Even if not at the Hôtel Régent, where I had dashed one more time on my bicycle and exchanged a few words with the pale receptionist with the nimble fingers. Even if not beneath the arcades of the rue de Rivoli, where I happened to see her at regular intervals. Even if not at the cramped café in front of the theatre, where she drank coffee with some stoutish Italian woman after morning rehearsals. Even if not at the pharmacy on the corner of the rue du Louvre, in the avenues of the Tuileries, in front of the Jeu de Paume . . . Even if only so she would tell me to my face that she didn't want to have anything more to do with me, and that was that.

"You're spying on her!" Lieutenant-Colonel Haas exclaimed.

"I'm spying on her, Little Prince," I echoed.

I even opened an atlas. My finger crossed the Italian border and plunged into the soft-green colour of her country. So that's where that Slovenia of hers is, I said to myself, I, who had never given much thought to my origins or looked at the borders of the country I live in. That green area around my finger. I tried to pronounce the names of the places I came across: Koper, Piran, Portorož . . . Postojna . . . and then Ljubljana. Lju-blja-na is her town. At least that's what she said. Ljubljana, I repeated.

15

No, we spoke to each other in French. Those first three weeks in Paris, of course, we did not speak. Those first three weeks in Paris she did not want to see me. In the Hôtel Régent she walked past me again as if we did not know one another, as if I were just one of the anonymous guests waiting for his wife who has forgotten God knows what in their room. And in the café near the theatre she turned the other way when she caught sight of me at the counter. I even had the impression that she rolled her eyes, as if to say: What the hell does he want from me? Doesn't he get it, or do I have to paint him a picture? Why doesn't he just go after other women – or rather men – and leave me alone?

In Madrid, and later in Paris, Sežana and Ljubljana we spoke French. In Milan we slipped into Italian from time to time, particularly when she was in the grip of exuberant cheerfulness and mimicry. In Sežana she put Slovene words in my mouth: *lastovka . . . dolina . . . morje . . . vino . . . kaj boš . . .* She was very much a polyglot. You'll tell me that all opera singers are polyglots. That may be so, but not like Lea Kralj. Lea Kralj heard every sound and could repeat it flawlessly. Had Janáček heard her pronounce *červenoučka, modroučka, žlutoučka,* he would not have believed his ears. The same could be said for Puccini, Bizet, even Strauss, though obviously with the help of Madame Kudelka . . . But stop me if I'm going on. Once I start going on about her linguistic ability there's really no stopping me. Or her way of expressing herself. Fast but precise, and in such a way that her words were detached from one another, surprised, as if this were the first time they found themselves in such a combination. Even when she said something quite ordinary or banal like: "Do I have to tell you everything all over again?" or "Open your ears, my accidental friend!" – I always had the impression that it was the first time I was hearing such words.

Or her way of expressing herself. For instance, Lea Kralj would often say such things as "indeed". (Your amnesia. Amnesia, indeed! Foolishness. Foolishness, indeed!) "The cream in my coffee". (You're the cream in my coffee, she once said.) Or "peace in Bosnia". (A peculiar idiom, now already an archaism, which was used in Slovenia and meant something like: Enough! Let's not talk about it any more!) And particularly, "Do I have to paint you a picture?" (When she was surprised, when she had to tell me something all over again, when I drove her to desperation.)

And then there was the meaning certain words had for her. Let's take the word "love", for instance. For her the word "love" was not passion between two people who love one another, for example between a man and a woman in her case, or between a man and a man in mine. For her, the word "love" was connected to something distant, past, cold, or not cold but wintry, and above all something linked to Madame Ingrid, her mother. But I'll tell you about that later.

16

I will also reply to your question about her headscarf later, when I tell you about the New Year's Eve concert in Milan. I think you have altogether the wrong idea about her headscarf. And not only about her headscarf, now that we're on the subject. The reason Lea Kralj wore a headscarf was not because, like other opera singers, she feared the slightest breeze, draught, chill, complications of the ear, nose, or throat. She didn't wear it out of coquetry either, or, God forbid, because of some fetishistic tendency.

Even if, and I'm telling the truth, headscarves really suited her. Just look at any of the photos in which she is wearing a headscarf. The one of her in Paris, for instance, in front of the Bastille during the rehearsals for *Katya Kabanova*, where she is in three-quarters profile with one hand resting on her shoulder, and wearing a sleeveless print dress. No, you can't actually see the print dress. In the deep décolleté you can see the area of skin between her neck and the ends of the scarf hanging down to her breasts. You can see the clean oval of her face, the freckles near her nose and eyes. Her full lips with dimples at the corners of her mouth, the two light lines on her cheeks. And there is something touching, vulnerable, but also playful about her, a plant that has unexpectedly flowered out of season, and what a flower, if I may make another small botanical digression.

In a recent issue of *Petronius*, in the column "À la folie", we published a whole series of photographs under the heading "Prima Donna or Madonna?" in which she was wearing her headscarf: Lea Kralj in front of Café Puccini in Amsterdam, in the mirror of her Paris dressing room, from behind, barefoot on the beach at Barcelona, with open arms in a snowy Milan, and an extreme close-up on the Place de la Bastille. The headscarf stretches like a red thread, a strange obsession, stylishly, a single fashion accessory, my compliments, Madame!

But Lea Kralj was always trying not to wear her headscarf. Every new day without it was like some sort of victory for her. Back then, of course, I couldn't have known that. The pale receptionist with the nimble fingers had been right.

17

She became known as "The Prima Donna who knows how to die" only after *Tosca*. More likely than not it was Lluis Toronto who had a hand in the matter. He built a whole theory around her ability, her gift, of dying on stage, as he put it. I am sure he would be willing to tell you all about it. As you can see, I am telling another story, which unfortunately also has to do with death, a story that happened in real life and not on stage. Furthermore, I've never had all that much to do with opera and am far from being a *folle lyrique* . . . I don't know how you would translate that into Slovene. *Folles lyriques* are homosexuals who are crazy about opera and obsessed with prima donnas, whom they love passionately but chastely. I became interested in Lea Kralj, who happened to be both a prima donna and a Slovenian. "Interested" is of course not the best word. Our story, at times not at all chaste, would have been precisely the same had Lea Kralj been . . . well, a pharmacist, for instance, or a singer in the chorus. At least that's my impression. I would still have taken her on my bicycle, I would still have walked with her kilometre after kilometre, she would still have waited for me at the train station in Trieste. And I would still have become involved with her lover Remek, not to mention her mother Ingrid.

But since we are on the subject, I will quote an article from one of the women's magazines that came out a few days before her première (with that close-up of her I've already mentioned that was taken in front of the Bastille), which looks at the matter from a different viewpoint, at least that's my impression. It is signed with the initials M. C. – I actually know it by heart, particularly the last two sentences, which I still often quote as if it were a long prose poem.

"We see her from a distance. From a distance nobody would think that we have a prima donna before us. This tall, blond young woman is dressed like you or me in a short skirt, a dark jacket with three-quarter sleeves, and wearing a silk head-scarf – the only unusual thing about her, particularly on such a sunny spring afternoon. From a distance she looks to us like a twin sister. Even when she sits down in an empty chair at a table and orders linden tea, it is hard to see in her the prima donna who in a few days will die for us. And that is precisely the role of opera singers, to die before our eyes evening after evening: Violetta, Tosca, Mimi, Angelica, Katya. For when their voices rise or fall one last time as they encounter death on stage, we feel a sting in our hearts as if they were really dying. As if they were also dying for us, so that then, with moist eyes, we can leave the theatre for daily life, where love or hate are never so strong that one is ready to die for them."

18

To clarify matters, it was Lluis Puig Xirinacs (Toronto is his pseudonym) who spoke about the food poisoning, and also the bathrooms. Over time, Lea Kralj had become his diva, his trophy. Professionally, of course, though he had no qualms about mixing professional and private matters. In Paris he bought her *marrons glacés*, all kinds of books, invited her to dinner, to the cinema, to art exhibitions. Business dinners, business screenings, and even business art exhibitions, he stressed, tapping his pencil. Opera, after all, is a fusion of all the arts. Lea Kralj frequently accepted his invitations, though she generally turned them down, telling him she had an appointment with Madame Kudelka, which usually was true enough. During the period of her brief affair with one of the electricians, who took their lightning sexual encounters as a sign of personal promotion and began spreading indiscreet details about her in the corridors, Toronto did everything in his power to suppress rumours such as: Lea Kralj likes doing it standing, quickly, as if a fire has been lit under her . . . Lea Kralj has the habit of bursting into tears after an orgasm . . . Have you ever heard of anything like that before? As if I hadn't made love to her, but beaten her . . .

Toronto can surely supply all the details. He might well publish one of his famous diaries, as he always keeps one for each of his productions, a *carnet de route*, as he calls them, where everything is noted down from beginning to end. Her difficulty in concentrating, for instance, where to stand, where to enter and where to exit . . . or what to do with the basket of flowers . . . Toronto was obsessed with that basket. A few flowers in a woven basket were to be a symbol of Katya Kabanova's connection to nature, the same flowers that we see scattered over the Volga at the end, as with Ophelia, for Katya's death resembles that of Ophelia, and so on . . . But also Lea Kralj's humming. She always hummed tunes before going on stage or during intermissions. According to Toronto, that was one of her characteristics. Humming light melodies in her dressing room, in the corridors, in the wings, *che non si muore per amore è una gran bella verità* . . . and then plunging into the opera.

And especially the precise flow of the rehearsals, day after day. At the end of April, a few days before the first rehearsal in costume with piano accompaniment, she had food poisoning. In the middle of the afternoon rehearsals with the pianist, she suddenly turned white, gasped, and doubled over.

"Is something wrong?" the Italian woman singing the role of Varvara asked.

"I think I'm going to be sick," Lea Kralj said in a choking voice, and hurried to the toilet, still doubled over.

The scene repeated itself every afternoon. After the first half hour of rehearsal, during which one might think that her nausea had disappeared overnight, her cheeks once again a healthy red and her voice ready as always, she suddenly fell silent as if she couldn't breathe, turned white, and doubled over.

47

"I can't go on, I can't," she whispered desperately, as Toronto, the singers, and the pianist crowded around her. Varvara splashed water on her forehead and stroked her hair.

"It'll pass," she assured her.

"It won't! Who said it would? It won't pass!" Lea Kralj said over and over. Toronto had Doctor Molino brought in, a mild-mannered man with drooping shoulders and a snow-white mane. He examined her, wrote her a prescription for nausea, and the same afternoon sent her to a laboratory for a blood test. The following morning she dragged herself to the rehearsal. Molina dropped by around noon and announced that according to the initial analysis she had food poisoning. Lea Kralj sat slumped in her chair, as if they were talking about someone else.

"Food poisoning?" she repeated in disbelief.

There was silence. Toronto took a deep breath and hid his face in his hands.

"Are you sure?"

"Absolutely," the doctor replied, taking some papers out of his bag. "Needless to say, if you doubt my word we can always do more tests," he added.

"Oh, no, no," Lea Kralj said, seizing him by the wrists. "Of course I believe you. You can't imagine how I believe you!"

19

It's not that she really had a thing about bathrooms, even if it might seem so at first glance. In every new hotel room, she always looked at the bathroom first. Bathrooms were one of the few things that could make her suddenly aggressive, testy, even insulting. You call this a bathroom? Because if you think that this is a bathroom, that means you don't have a single bathroom in your hotel! Do you even know what the word "bathroom" means? *Salle de bains, cuarto de baño, Badezimmer, bagno*! She put her hands on her hips and raised her eyes to heaven. She was prepared to sleep in any kind of hotel – shabby, snobbish, somewhere in the outskirts – as long as she could have a bathroom. What *she* called a bathroom.

A bathroom is a big room that (this is important!) does not look out onto the street. A bathroom has a high ceiling and ceramic tiles everywhere. A bathroom has a big tub. A mirror is essential, a mirror that is as large as possible, or at least large enough to see one's whole torso. Just as important is the anonymous towelling hotel dressing-gown, though this comes last on her list. All the rest – bidet, hairdryer, and toiletries provided by the hotel, such as soap, shampoo, toothbrush, and plastic shower cap – didn't interest her at all. She always threw these in the dustbin.

What did she do in bathrooms?

Bathed, like anyone else, let the taps run at full blast, and, above all, sang.

20

Of course you are right: I'd never have thought that one day I would be telling this story the way I am now. Slovenia's Woman of 2000! A poetess, a long-distance runner, a social worker, a television celebrity – and Lea Kralj! One question after another. As if I were walking, one step after another. I hope you have noticed that I am doing my best to keep the events in some kind of chronological order: Madrid, Paris, Milan, and later Sežana and Ljubljana. To unravel the red thread of our story. Though the story is not just ours alone. The main protagonists, whichever way you look at it, are Lea Kralj and her mother Madame Ingrid. I am only the chronicler, or a minor character, if you will. A minor character who from time to time steps into the foreground. A minor character who could have saved her life. A minor character who even today cannot forget what happened. But back then I would have never even dreamt of such a thing.

Back then, in those first days of May to be precise, I had decided to go past the Hôtel Régent one last time. It was mid-afternoon, a nervous wind was blowing. I leaned my bicycle against the metal fence across from the hotel and went through the glass door, out of breath. The pale receptionist with the nimble fingers again had her hands full: in one hand she was holding the phone, while the fingers of the other were drumming on the counter. When she saw me, she nodded in the direction of the empty sofa behind the first Greek column, and motioned me to take a seat. She was wearing her hair up, with wayward ringlets tumbling over her temples. She was wearing a ring in the form of a watch on her middle finger. I nodded to indicate that I didn't want to trouble her, not in the least. Had she not been so engrossed in her interlocutor's monologue and her free hand so busy, I would have turned around and left. I had no business being in that lobby. I had nothing to say, I wasn't waiting for anyone, nor was I bringing anyone a message. Let us just say that I simply wanted to take one last look at that lobby with its replica of a row of Greek columns, its large Persian carpet, its velvet sofas, and the symmetrically arranged table lamps with shades from which different coloured silk pompoms were hanging. And also to say goodbye to the Slovenian prima donna. To tell myself that we had crossed paths in the middle of Madrid, that I had crossed hers backstage at the Zarzuela and she had crossed mine in the Calle de la Cabeza late at night, on the edge of consciousness . . . but without any of this having particular significance, a fact that she too gave me to understand when she walked past me as if she didn't know me. To each his own, young man. I will continue singing Angelica, Katya, Mimi, Tosca . . . and you . . . you can do whatever you like, yes, whatever you like. If the pale receptionist had not clung to the unknown voice on the phone so persistently, and if her fingers had not drummed so evenly on the counter – was there really someone on the other end, I wondered – I would have turned around, perhaps even nodded at the young woman with the nimble fingers, and taken the few steps that would have made the glass doors open before me of their own accord.

Naturally, now that I know the course of events, it is easy enough to speculate. To think that perhaps there wasn't really anyone on the other end of the kind receptionist's line. That she was only holding the receiver to her ear, that her fingers were drumming on the counter in front of her, and that she was paying no attention to me, as I gazed blankly at the entrance, the columns, the lamps, the pompoms . . . And that in this way she gave Lea enough time to step out of the lift, fix her shoe, come directly towards me, and say with a calm voice, in a way that the words broke away from one another: "Ah, there you are. As if I'd snapped my fingers. At the perfect moment."

21

And she did step out of the lift. She bent one leg, raising it, arched her back like a ballerina, and did fix her shoe. She looked rested and fresh, as if she had just woken up, slipped into her patterned skirt and black jacket and, without even combing her hair or looking in the mirror, left the room. She was holding her headscarf and sunglasses in one hand. Then she really did move, really did walk towards me. Really did say, quietly and with barely perceptible spaces between her words: "Ah, there you are. As if I'd snapped my fingers. At the perfect moment."

I took a step back – or rather forwards – towards the door.

"Well, thank you very much!" I answered sharply.

She turned to the receptionist, who finally hung up and whispered a whole sentence of which I only understood the word "Christine".

"What's the thank you for?" she asked me in surprise, as she followed me out the glass doors.

"Wasn't I here last time 'as if you'd snapped your fingers'? Or the time before?" I called to her from the other side of the street, as I unlocked my bicycle and waited for her to cross.

"Oh, another little interview?" she asked gravely, though her lips were suppressing a smile.

"Why not?"

"Still a journalist?"

"You haven't answered my question," I said.

"Your memory is in top shape today. And so is mine, as you will see. But for that you'll have to come with me: straight ahead, over the bridge, and a little way beyond. We can do our interview along the way," she continued in the same grave tone, and I was still under the impression that she was making fun of me.

We walked in step with each other. I was pushing my bicycle with one hand, staring silently in front of me. She was as tall as me, took large steps, and carried her round breasts proudly.

"I have no idea what's going on, or where we're going," I said finally.

"Ask me something else. Do I know Janáček or Puccini? How is my repertoire doing? Is it still blank, as you put it in Madrid?" she said, looking at me from the corner of her eye. We walked onto the bridge.

"I thought you were interested in opera," she murmured when we were almost halfway across and I still hadn't replied.

"I'm interested in you," I said.

"In me?"

"Yes."

"Because of the roses and all that?"

53

"Because of the roses and all that."

"So what would you like to know?" she asked when we had almost reached the other side.

"Everything."

"Everything?"

"Yes. Like why you avoid me, for instance."

"Ask me something else."

"I won't."

"Please."

"What do you do when you're not rehearsing?"

"I walk."

"You walk?"

"Yes, I walk. Like I'm doing now with you. What else?"

"Did you really have food poisoning?"

"Food poisoning?" she said, stopping and grabbing hold of my bicycle with both hands. "I poisoned myself. With fear. I hadn't been so frightened in years. Of everything. The role of Katya . . . the black hole in front of me . . . Paris . . . Every day I told myself this was the end. That I would give up. That I would announce to the world that I couldn't go on. That I was frightened, that fear was grabbing me by the throat and twisting my stomach. The director called a doctor. The doctor knew right away what was going on. But he still did a blood test, and the next day announced at the rehearsal that I had food poisoning, but that the worst was over and that I would be fully recovered soon enough. I couldn't believe my ears."

She sighed and ran her hand over her neck. I had never heard her say so much about herself. Then she came closer to me. We walked beside each other in silence. She stopped in front of a building on the first corner after the bridge and looked up. "Wait for me here. I'll be right back," she said, and disappeared through glass doors that bore the sign "Medical Laboratory". She came back carrying an open envelope.

"One last question," she said breathlessly. "Ask me my blood-group."

She bit her lip and again looked at the piece of paper she had taken out of the envelope.

"Well, go on, what are you waiting for?" she said impatiently.

I leaned my bicycle against the nearest wall, crossed my arms, and asked what her blood-group was.

"B-positive," she replied, and then added: "Now you know."

22

Let us say that this was our secret code, our sign of brotherhood, our invisible stamp, like the one I got a while ago on the back of my hand when I left some gallery opening or other for half an hour, and when I came back they used a special camera to see if it was me, really me, if they could see the stamp. "B-positive" would be stamped on the backs of our hands.

Or to put it differently: if I could do it again, up to this point I wouldn't change anything. I would again go to the Hôtel Régent and walk up and down in front of the inscrutable receptionist, Christine. I would walk over the bridge again and wait outside the medical laboratory. When she would tell me she was hungry, that she hadn't eaten anything since breakfast, I would again nod towards my bicycle the way I had done. I would remain indifferent to all her wavering and doubts ("Can you imagine me on that bicycle, me? I've never ridden through Paris on a bicycle," and so on), until suddenly, when I least expected it, she would take those few steps that separated us, stand on tiptoe, and climb up onto my bicycle. See, that was easy enough, I would say and begin to pedal. See, that was easy enough, I would shout a few more times into the wind and laugh out loud. How easy. Who'd have thought? Unbelievable, the Little Prince would say. He'd never have thought it possible. That I would be carrying the Slovenian prima donna on my old Motobécane. That the Left Bank would flit by, the flower market, the Conciergerie to our left, the Pont Neuf, the Samaritaine, the Louvre, the Tuileries to our right . . . That above us the first stars would begin to twinkle, and that the thin sickle of the moon would rise just over the Grand Palais . . . That the same wind would beat against our faces . . . That her patterned dress would flap around my legs . . . That I would feel her body close to mine, rigid with discomfort, fear, the wind, and my zigzagging between cars . . . That I would try to amuse her, ask what she would like to eat, whisper the most diverse dishes into her ear: mushrooms with red radishes, potatoes in beer à la Flamande, black mussels in asparagus sauce, eel with exquisite sausages, all prepared in the kitchen of my friend, Chef Gian-Paolo. That I had suggested we drop in at his place, his kitchen looking out on a real garden with a real cherry tree. I would even explain that Gian-Paolo is a chef with two Michelin stars, and my ex . . . how else can I put it, my ex, whose bed has been closed to me for a long time now, but at whose table there is always a place or two set for me, and what a meal!

And when later (after having emptied our plates, and what dishes Gian-Paolo had prepared for us in his long and narrow kitchen!), I would walk past Gian-Paolo with a cup of coffee in each hand and he would ask who was the woman I was with, I would again stop in front of him, put the cups down on his counter and, like him, look out the window. Lea Kralj would again be standing by one of the trees at the corner of the garden by the neighbour's house. No, not standing, she would be leaning against it as if she were lying back on the lower part of the inclining trunk. She would be propping herself up with her legs on the ground, her hands would be resting on her stomach, her face would be turned to the sky. She would remain completely motionless, as if asleep.

"She is my prima donna," I would reply.

Gian-Paolo would go back to filling the snail shells with a light-green paste.

"Your prima donna!" he would exclaim theatrically, and click his tongue. "Who would have expected something like that? Life is full of surprises. Congratulations!" he would say, and with a flourish of his middle finger shove the delicious filling into the snail's interior.

It was only on another occasion, which had nothing to do with Chef Gian-Paolo, that I suddenly understood what my former lover with the two Michelin stars was hinting at. And on that occasion I finally realised that he was, in fact, right. Lea Kralj was my first woman. The first woman I rode with on my bicycle and introduced to Gian-Paolo (that goes without saying). The first woman with whom I shared the same blood-group (as you already know). The first woman I gazed at meticulously and with pleasure (with more meticulousness and pleasure than I gazed at myself). The first woman I regularly interviewed (though usually for personal ends). The first woman who could do a perfect imitation of me (which wasn't always particularly pleasant). The first woman about whose family I was more informed than I was about my own (not surprising, as I didn't really have one). The first woman I lived with in the same flat (but more about that later). The first woman I shared a lover with (more about that later too). A prima donna who would forever be my only prima donna. ("One never knows," my Little Prince would say, in response to which I would most resolutely shake my head.)

23

Katya Kabanova was in every way a great success. A personal success along the lines: From this day forth there is only one Katya – Lea Kralj! Sir Charles Mackerras kissed her hand in front of everyone. The first violinist discreetly dabbed his eyes. Roses rained down on her. No-one can die on stage as masterfully as Lea Kralj, one of the critics wrote. It took Toronto a long time to get over the triumph. I am sure he will describe it to you in great detail. Nothing pleases him more. The opportunity to speak about Katya. The obsession with repeating things. The première of *Katya Kabanova* in Paris. To relive that evening. From the beginning, from the first notes of the overture. From the first shudder. From the first feeling of something ripping: Imagine a piece of cloth, he will tell you – Toronto likes to express himself in metaphors – tearing in small bursts before your very eyes. Centimetre by centimetre. As if your insides were ripping too, he will tell you. And those rips are so unexpected, so spontaneous, so unannounced, one after another, that they don't even have the chance to surface and establish themselves as a feeling. *Katya Kabanova*, he will tell you, is this continuing sensation of ripping inside you, without respite, without relief. Until the final bang, the final shudder, until the end. Until her death, he will tell you. Until the final note. And even after that. Until the velvet curtain comes down. And even after that. Until those few, infinite, interstellar seconds of silence before the audience explodes. Thousands and thousands of hands clapping against each other. Until the velvet curtain moves. One arm, a second arm . . . a spotlight . . . And then the prima donna, Lea Kralj, he will tell you. Sallow, exhausted, alone. *Bravissima!* bursts from the audience.

I wasn't there. Haas had called me that afternoon. He sounded determined. I jumped into the first taxi. When I arrived at his place, I found him lounging in an armchair in a deep lethargy. Three covers pulled up to his chin. Dark shadows beneath his feverish eyes. His hair even whiter than usual. Silent. Withdrawn. His dark-blue uniform with its air-force insignia hung apathetically in the wardrobe. There were a few cracked glasses and some bonbon-like pills on the table. It was only towards evening that he began to speak. He was shivering with cold and something like jealousy. I'm not important enough to you, he kept saying. I'm not number one. I placed my palm on his damp stomach. With this gesture he calmed down a little. And as I touched him, I realised for the first time that my life and hers were entwined. That from now on, come what may, I was linked to her. That Lieutenant-Colonel Haas, alias the Little Prince, might have managed to stop me from attending the première of *Katya Kabanova*. But that my hand on his stomach felt her shudders . . . Like the shudders that Toronto enjoys talking about so much. For what happens to her happens to me too. What hurts her hurts me too. Back then I believed that this connection to her was possible.

24

I do not know where you got the idea that she was "modest". Why should she have been modest? Lea Kralj was not modest, as I am sure all the other contestants for Slovenia's Woman of 2000 must be (except for the television celebrity and perhaps the long-distance runner).

Lea Kralj wanted everything. To sing in the biggest opera houses, with the greatest conductors, orchestras, directors, set designers, lighting technicians . . . To fascinate the public, have it under her spell, draw tears from people's eyes . . . But also to make her public laugh, or to startle it as she startled me, for instance, when she did one of her imitations of me, which I will have to go into another time; to experience stage fright, even the dreadful fear that twisted her stomach and wouldn't let her breathe. But to overcome that fear, to find in herself the courage she did not have, precisely that: finding in oneself the courage one does not have, stepping out onto the stage, feeling the air in one's lungs, a lot of air, and one's voice that comes from deep inside, from near the uterus and ovaries, as she told me during one of our walks. To sing Janáček, Puccini too, of course, but also Rossini – why not? To wear beautiful dresses, even though she did not know how to dress (that is, in the sense of what I mean by knowing how to dress). To go out to dinners, even though afterwards she usually would not eat for two days in order to counterbalance all the good food. To buy black lace lingerie. To have men when she was in the mood. To have her own director, who saw himself as her Pygmalion. Even to have her own official accompanist . . . To drink wine with her Slovenian neighbour Drago, to sit with him silently in the yard . . . To play the piano when she wanted to play the piano. To drive around in her Toyota. To have her house, her trees, even her beans . . . To not wear her headscarf. Lea Kralj wanted everything, but more than anything she wanted the love of her mother, Madame Ingrid.

25

Some people, Lieutenant-Colonel Haas, for instance, called her "the Slovenian". "How's the Slovenian doing?" he would ask. With that he maintained his distance from her. Often I could even sense a touch of something resembling irony. He'd hand me the phone and say: "It's the Slovenian". Or he would ask: "So did you have a pleasant evening with the Slovenian?" Or: "What do you see in the Slovenian?"

Sometimes I actually tried to respond. I too had wondered what Pablo Ortez had seen in Marta, that moon-faced translator. Every few days she would ring the door-bell of the Divino bookshop, stand on her toes, and rest her cheek on his neck, or lean forwards, her pouting lips ready for a kiss. She would just plump herself down on a step in front of the bookshelves, cross her short little thighs, light a cigarette, and make herself at home. Or what had Pablo seen in Cecilia, the photographer with the generous breasts and the irrefutable talent? Or pitiful Ana-María with her chronic asthma that seized her even when she was in Pablo's arms, so that one windy night I ended up having to call the doctor while Pablo caressed her hands and soothed her. Or Sybil, whom I do not even really remember. Or Nieves, irrelevant Nieves, who supposedly shared his passion for botany. Not to mention Señora García Fernández who, judging by her radiant complexion on Wednesday evenings when she slipped out of the Divino through the back door, had to be one of his most adept sex partners.

I've never met an opera singer before – I said to the Little Prince – not to mention a Slovenian. Or: I like the way she walks, the way she cuts through the air, so lithe. She could be an athlete, perhaps a long-jumper. Or: The freckles, there are a few yellowish freckles beneath her eyes. Or simply: I don't know, I really don't know. Sometimes I wonder too.

62

When he asked me, the day before the final performance of *Katya Kabanova*, when the Slovenian was leaving, and I told him that this was her last day in Paris, he gave a sigh of relief. And that evening, after she had checked out of the Hôtel Régent and he asked if she had finally left, I said yes.

What else could I have said? That the Slovenian always makes the ground beneath my feet shake, that she doesn't do things like anyone else, not even something as simple as saying goodbye, farewell, adieu, keep well, don't forget me . . . That she and I had ended up together in front of the Hôtel Régent waiting for her taxi. A warm, windless night was coming on, and the stench of smog was stronger than usual. The sky behind the Tuileries began to turn vivid colours. The Slovenian was wearing a sleeveless muslin summer dress and her headscarf with the birds, tied at the nape of her neck. I looked at her out of the corner of my eye. She really was pretty in that summery dress that was a little out of fashion, like most of her clothes, not quite modish, but which somehow hung softly about her. She was pretty, with those long, soft arms of hers and even with that headscarf tied at the nape. Had I been a passer-by, I would probably have turned around to look at her, I would have told myself that she had to be from another world or something like that – I always turn around and look at people who catch my attention one way or another. She stared silently in front of her, at the cars that were tearing past along the Rue de Rivoli, as if she were weighing what she was going to say in the few moments before the taxi arrived. I, too, tried to put together something to say.

Something along the lines that we already had two metropolises behind us, and not just any metropolises, but Madrid and Paris! And that the easiest thing would be to continue this way, now that we had started – what did she think? The world is big and it belongs to us. Anyway, I wish you a good trip, or simply all the best! At that moment the taxi pulled up. "At last!" she said, fed up with waiting, and leaned down to the driver. She probably hadn't been intending to say anything to me, and had only been staring blankly at the passing cars, I thought. We put her bags in the boot. As she opened the door of the taxi, she nodded one last time to Christine, the receptionist, who for once was not on the phone and was watching us through the glass doors, and then mumbled something at me that I didn't catch. So although she was already in the taxi and had closed the door, I leaned down towards her. With her breath she fogged up the glass that was separating us and drew "B+" with her finger.

26

Now I see everything that happened as a single, long journey towards Ljubljana. Madrid, Paris, Milan, Sežana, Ljubljana. Madrid, Paris, Milan, Sežana are stations along the route to the terminus, last stop, Ladies and Gentlemen! Everybody got off, one after another, Remek, me, Haas, Pablo, Kudelka, Ingrid . . .

Pablo was the first to get off. He was run over by a car. In the middle of Madrid, towards the end of summer, on an evening very much like our last evening together in the Parque del Retiro, Cecilia the photographer told me on the phone. Cecilia obviously didn't actually say to me "on an evening very much like your last evening together" . . . Cecilia said that towards evening Pablo was on his way back from the Divino on foot, a newspaper under his arm, as was his habit (the two top buttons of his checked shirt open, I thought, and with that triangle of damp skin below his throat). No-one knew exactly how it happened. The driver, a young man wearing red trousers, gave his version: Pablo was suddenly in front of him, in the middle of the street, in the most unlit part of the neighbourhood, as if somebody had just dropped him there. Pablo didn't say anything, Pablo only stared ahead. The people who came running, and later the ambulance team, thought he would walk away with a few bruises and a light concussion. He sat for a while on the pavement, leaning against the wall behind him, as if there were nothing wrong with him, as if he just needed to catch his breath a little, to rest. He even took out a cigarette and twirled it between his fingers without lighting it. Perhaps when he was told he couldn't sit there on the pavement, he might even have waved his hand and said: *Loquerías, tonterías* . . . When they insisted on taking him to the hospital, he was dead on arrival. He had died on the way, Cecilia said. A cerebral haemorrhage. He looked perfectly fine, she said. He looked just the way he always did, there were only a few small cuts and bruises on his chin and arms. That's Pablo for you! . . . You know what I mean, she said. I nodded into the emptiness. I hung up and stared into the mirror in front of me. I looked at myself for a long time, at my silvery reflection, a long time, until I saw Pablo's face instead of mine.

27

Absolutely not. Even if at times life seems a frightening, poisonous gift, it is out of the question! Though you could say that everyone's life is poisoned in a different way.

28

This isn't *one* of the photographs in which we are together. It is the only photograph in which we are together. Black-and-white, of the kind that newspapers and magazines like to print, with captions such as: Lea Kralj and her companion, Milan, 1997. Lea Kralj, smiling after her triumph in *Tosca*, accompanied by her young friend, December, 1997. Winter idyll between *Tosca* performances, Milan, 1997. The picture of happiness, a stone's throw from La Scala, 1997.

The photograph was taken after her last performance of *Tosca*, a few days before I arrived in Milan. Everything is in it: our street, Via Fiori Chiari, the café on the corner where we usually drank coffee or San Pelegrino, the pavement in front of it, the daily bouquet of white roses that an unknown admirer left on the doormat, her long brown coat, her thick gloves, my glasses. And snow, real snow, which had begun falling the evening my train pulled into the station at Milan.

Winter is my favourite time of year, Lea Kralj had said. That is why she had insisted that I come to end the year in Milan. That is why she wanted me to come at all costs, though she telephoned me at the last moment, regardless of whether I might have other plans. Her mother would be coming for New Year, so I would get to meet her. Lea Kralj had taken a large flat in the Via Fiori Chiari, and I was sure to like it. Three rooms, high ceilings, a balcony looking out on an inner courtyard, a real bathroom, a pleasant kitchen . . . We haven't seen each other for some time, she said, since Paris, if I recall . . . The year had flitted by so fast! And now that it had almost reached the finish line, now that *Tosca* was done with and only the New Year's Eve concert was left, and now that it had finally got cold again, we could spend a few days together, wait for her mother, what did I think?

I didn't think anything. Haas and I were intending to go to the seaside. But I didn't go to the seaside. A few days later I got on a train, and a few days after that I found myself in this photograph. In our only photograph together, and one of the few – look at it closely – in which Lea Kralj is smiling. Not only smiling, but cheerful, perhaps even happy. And I'm smiling too, not the way she is, but smiling, as I had no choice.

That morning, it was snowing for the third day in a row and we were to meet the photographer Fabrizio Borgese in front of our café, I discovered that Lea Kralj was a master at imitating people. Anybody. Our elegant neighbour on the third floor, Signora Einaudi, who flew off the handle at the least provocation, waving her wrist in spirals so that all her bracelets jangled, or Toronto with his pencil – you should have seen her, what a skit! – or a man in the street wearing hat and gloves with a scarf thickly wound around his neck. And above all, me. I was her foremost model. We were walking along the Via Fiori Chiari. Lejka (in Milan I began calling her Lejka) was telling me how and where she had met Fabrizio, the photographer. Suddenly she seemed preoccupied. A spark of light, or rather a flush, touched her cheeks. She grabbed the bouquet I was holding. She took off my glasses and put them on. She ruffled her hair with a delicate sweep of her hand, patting it down over her forehead and then parting it to the side. She drew out her lips into a sort of flat smile that probably doesn't even deserve to be called a smile. She made sure that the outfit was in order. Slipped her hand into her pocket. Raised her head like some skinny cockerel. Took a few mincing steps, her feet delicately touching the pavement. "Good God! Do I really walk like that? What would someone like you be doing with someone like me?" I mumbled in a state of shock. "Walking," she replied, trying to keep a straight face. Then she suddenly burst out laughing, raised her arms as if to thank the audience, Ladies and Gentlemen, end of skit . . . I smiled too – sourly, but I smiled. Then we saw Fabrizio Borgese standing a few feet away with his camera. He had obviously just pressed the shutter.

29

A little while ago, the editor of *Petronius* declared in his prissy, nasal voice that he only had one desire left in life: to live with an opera singer. We were sitting at a table in the editorial office. There was silence, as if something more important was to come. "What a delight! To wake up and hear 'Casta Diva'," he said, caressing his stomach.

I lived with an opera singer – and not just any opera singer – for exactly twelve and a half days. And yet in those twelve and a half days I never woke to the sounds of 'Casta Diva' or any other famous aria. First of all, because Lea Kralj always sang in the bathroom. And secondly, because when she wasn't singing in the bathroom, she sang everything except 'Casta Diva'. When she was cleaning the flat, especially when she was cleaning the flat. But also when she was washing her underwear, dressing, bathing . . . Even when she was thinking about something. You could see in her expression that her thoughts were straying God knows where, while her mouth was singing of its own accord: "*Che non si muore per amore è una gran bella verità*" . . . for instance. Or: *Quando ero piccola* . . . In restaurants, when her eyes ran over the menu, she would mumble sotto voce: *parole, parole, parole* . . . When she spread butter on her bread she sang: *Avec le temps, tout s'en va* . . . or: *Ne me quitte pas* . . . When she let down the blinds in her bedroom, she sang to the night: . . . *seguiremos adelante, hasta siempre Comandante* . . .

Her repertoire of Italian and French songs, even South American revolutionary ones, seemed inexhaustible. From time to time she also sang something Slovenian, sadder songs, at least that's how they seemed to me. I still remember the melody and also a few of the words, though I didn't understand them. But her language, and also a certain song about a nightingale I often heard her sing,

69

seemed ever closer to me – in some way I even understood it. *"Kaj jo je prignalo, od kod je le prišla čisto noter vate jokat lastovka,"* she would sing, and I heard the fluttering of wings in her voice.

30

Today I would say that it was in the third-floor flat of the Via Fiori Chiari that we really began to study one another, to get used to one another. Began to repeat certain patterns that were ours alone, patterns that gradually turned into something like a motif that kept reappearing in our scores. Today I believe that we all have motifs in our lives, which we repeat unconsciously and in different variations, like patterns on a piece of cloth. Her sitting by my bed, for instance. Nobody else sat by my bed the way Lea Kralj did. When she felt I had slept too long, which she felt often enough, she came in and woke me up. She would sit down at the head of my bed and wait for me to open my eyes. When I did, I saw hers above me, colourlessly patient but also surprised, even amazed, as if every morning she again found me lying in the street and wondered who I might be. She usually murmured something about my peaceful, even innocent sleep, and waited for me to wake up completely. Then she would leave the room on tiptoe. After all, my night of amnesia in Madrid had also ended with her face above mine, not to mention the unforgettable morning after the stormy night in Sežana.

I never walked with anyone the distances I walked with

her. Long walks with Lea Kralj. Walk straight ahead, always straight ahead, and more often than not you arrive somewhere, but walk on and on, even if you are at the end of your tether, wherever, whenever, in whatever weather, in Paris, Milan, Sežana, even Ljubljana. And then, when you feel that the road is endless, that it goes on, straight ahead or through detours, that it goes on and on, then you raise your hand, stop the first taxi that comes your way and climb into the back without a word, as if you had finally arrived at your destination.

And nobody ever greeted me the way she did with that "*ciao bello*" of hers, so that I could never tell if she really thought me "*bello*", or if she was just making fun of me in a nice way.

3 1

It was also in the Via Fiori Chiari that we grew closest to one another. We told each other so many things in the kitchen, at the table covered with a plastic tablecloth that had a design of nothing but green stems. Never again would we speak to one another in this way, openly, spontaneously, telling each other whatever came to mind. Even now I still remember some of our conversations, about Ingrid, an unavoidable subject, and also about Madame Kudelka, Haas, or my favourite topic: how things would be if they weren't the way they were.

"Who is Haas? Why do you call him 'Lieutenant-Colonel'," and why 'Little Prince'?" she asked me.

After that autumn in Madrid, I began, it was Haas's turn. After my goodbye to Pablo in the botanical gardens. When I saw Haas at the *métro* station, lean and tall, in his dark-blue air-force uniform, I had the urge to become someone's prey. His, for instance. That dark-blue uniform with gold insignia, and that tall bearing of his, struck me as quite a promising start. So there we were, riding on the Boulogne–Gare d'Austerlitz line. I casually sat down next to him and waited for him to take the initiative. He unfolded his newspaper and began to read. I could see his delicate hands with their golden hairs. His profile with its decisive chin. And – he had in the meantime taken off his cap and placed it on his knees under the newspaper – his thin hair that was entirely white. The more I looked at him, the more I wanted to become his prey. For a short while, but still his prey. Hypothetically, we had nine stations to go, that is, if we were both to stay on the train to the last stop, which was hardly likely. As I have already mentioned, I was waiting for him to make a move. But Haas does not launch offensives; he does not have a talent for operations. The only military tactics he is capable of are defence tactics. And I did not want to take the initiative. No slight touch of thigh or shoulder, no sign, nothing. What will be will be. I peered over at his newspaper. That was as far as I was prepared to go. And I even began to read it, which I often do – reading a newspaper over the shoulder of the person next to me in the *métro*. I still remember: "Woody Allen was as good as his word and married his stepdaughter, Soon Yi . . . And not just anywhere, but in Venice . . . So that nobody who might object to the wedding would be present . . . Morality prevails, love knows no boundaries . . . The mayor of Venice married them in person . . . Then they left for . . ." The train arrived at the last stop. Haas folded his paper and turned towards the doors, which opened wide before us.

"Then they left for . . ." I said, despite myself, repeating the last line I had seen in his paper.

Haas stopped in his tracks. He looked at me in surprise, thankfully, even smiled sheepishly. His eyes were bluer than Pablo's, and there was something spacious about his look, something reminiscent of hospitals . . . long hospital corridors . . . Eyes that you sink into, lose your way in . . . We got off the train and took the escalator up to the street. He was almost half a head taller than me. We didn't say a word all the way to his flat. What should we have talked about? In his living room we undressed in silence. In the early twilight I saw his wonderful *ricardo* . . .

"*Ricardo?*" she asked. She peeked under the table, below my belt.

"That's right," I said.

"And then?"

"We read no further."

32

"Why did you say it was Haas's turn?" she asked after a few moments.

"How should I have put it?"

"I don't know. It sounds a little mechanical."

"Mechanical?"

73

"Yes. But also puckish. Nonchalant. Debonair. Mr Casanova junior."

"Don't exaggerate," I said.

"Who's exaggerating?"

"I don't get what you are saying. Do you disapprove?"

"No. Not at all. Quite the opposite," she said, and rested her chin on top of her hands that were lying on the table, so that she looked up at me crookedly.

"Quite the opposite?"

"Yes. It looks like you and I have something in common."

"In common?" I said in amazement.

"You haven't told me why you call him 'Little Prince'," she continued.

"Because he keeps asking one question after another," I said, which was obviously no answer. I should have said: because he flies a plane, because he has white hair, blue eyes, golden hairs on his hands, and so on. And above all, because Pablo hated the Little Prince. I mean the book, with all its candy-coated pseudo-naiveté and pseudo-poetry, foxes, roses, stargazers, *dessine-moi un mouton* . . . But at that moment I didn't want to talk about all this, in other words to bring up Pablo's name in connection with Haas.

33

I wanted to know why we were waiting so impatiently for Madame Ingrid, her mother. Why all the preparations? The cleaning of the flat that wasn't even hers, that she had only rented for a short period. The Christmas tree we had bought but not yet decorated. The new towels in the bathroom. Her mother might have deigned to grace us with her presence a little earlier, didn't she think? For the *Tosca* performance, perhaps. She should be proud of her daughter, the way I am, who am only her – how should one put it? – her dedicated observer.

"She couldn't come," Lea said, getting up and clearing the plates from the table. Suddenly, and for no reason, she opened the dishwasher, loudly slammed it shut, and began cleaning the oven.

"Come and sit down."

She looked at me over her shoulder without answering. She continued cleaning the oven meticulously, rinsed her hands for a long time, dried them for a long time on a kitchen towel, and then finally turned and faced me.

"Ingrid is very busy. You cannot imagine how busy she is. She's just begun a series of lectures on medicinal and poisonous plants. Every week another lecture . . . For an association of retired physicians, or something of the sort . . . But word has got around, and now all kinds of people come to her lectures who are neither doctors nor retired."

"You don't say!"

She leaned against the oven, still holding the kitchen towel in her hand. She was wearing a long nightgown and woollen socks. With the towel in her hands, there was suddenly something helpless, even funny, about her that made you want to hug her, take the towel out of her hands, and throw it in the rubbish.

"You do say!" I said playfully, trying to brighten her mood a little.

But that morning she was in no mood to laugh. I barely managed to drag anything out of her. Madame Ingrid did not seem to be following her daughter's career all that closely. Once, many years ago, she had come to stay, when Lejka was living in Paris and taking voice lessons with Madame Kudelka while doing odd jobs on the side, even teaching Italian, among other things. Lejka had been as excited as a child. At last! she had said to herself. At last my mother is coming! At last she will see how I live! She would show her mother Paris. Take her to the shops. Cater to her every whim. They would eat in restaurants. But Madame Ingrid got an upset stomach. After two days she went back to Ljubljana. Those French don't know how to cook, were her parting words.

34

On another morning – it had been snowing for three days in a row and we had an appointment with Fabrizio Borgese near our corner café – she told me about a winter when she was a child that had been incomparably colder. It had been so cold that all the houses had icicles and frost-covered windows, the ground had creaked beneath one's feet, there wasn't a living soul to be seen except for her mother, her sister, and herself, she told me. Ingrid was not afraid of the cold. She dressed her daughters warmly – hats, gloves, boots – and drove them to the nearby hill. On the path through the woods she put the youngest on the ground: the little girl traipsed through the snow, scooping it up in her arms. The older girl,

Lejka, walked in front, also scooping up the hard snow and studying the imprint she made . . . Until her gloves were wet, until they were stiff with cold and her hands began to freeze more than she could say . . . and so on, as you already know. Her distant memory, which with time has become mine too.

"That seems a very effective way of warming someone's hands!" I said in surprise when she came to the part where her mother had clasped her little hands and put them in her mouth.

"Ingrid is always effective. Whatever she does," she told me, her lips curling into a sweet smile, behind which I saw a touch of irony.

"I can believe that. I saw her reduce you to tears in the twinkling of an eye," I said in the same tone.

"What are you talking about?" she asked, taken aback.

"In Madrid, when you hung up."

"In Madrid, when I hung up?"

"Don't you remember? You were about to leave when the phone rang. You began to talk, and then suddenly . . ."

"That was my fault," she said. "I had bought her a present she didn't like. I should have known she wouldn't like it. Ingrid never wears watches."

"Why in God's name are you so obsessed with pleasing her?" I whispered, as if my voice had left me.

"What do you mean?"

"Everything," I said, and looked around as if I was about to find an example of "everything".

"Because she's my mother," she interrupted me unconvincingly, and above all in a way that made it clear that this was her last word on the subject.

35

"I think I was also afraid of her," she told me another time, at that same table with the green stems.

"Afraid of whom?"

"Ingrid."

"Of Ingrid?"

"Yes. I think I was afraid of her, but at the same time also proud."

"Why?" I asked, even though I knew she was going to continue. In those few days I had learned to read in her face the rare moments in which she was ready, to some extent, to confide in me.

"Once one of my classmates at school – Robi, his name was Robi – asked me what my father did for a living," she began. "'I don't know,' I told him. Which was quite true. My father had divorced my mother and left for Brazil when I was seven. No, he actually left and got a divorce later. Either way, I really had no idea what he was doing in Brazil, especially as Ingrid did not want us to talk about him at home. 'Why don't you know what his job is?' Robi had wondered. I told him: 'My mother is an anaesthesiologist.' 'What's an anaesthesiologist?' he wanted to know. And I told him: 'An anaesthesiologist is someone who can make you go to sleep so deep that you die, if she wants to, and who can wake you up again, if she wants to.' Robi opened his eyes wide. A couple of days later he asked me if my mother was still . . . an anaesthesiologist. 'Yes, she is,' I had answered proudly."

36

"What would you be if you weren't an opera singer?"

"What a question! I'll have to watch my p's and q's!"

"Go on, tell me!"

She was again rummaging about in the kitchen. She was standing in front of the oven and then darted behind me, covering my eyes with her hands before I knew what she was doing.

"What would you see now if I wasn't covering your eyes?" she said, imitating my voice.

"Go on, tell me," I insisted, blowing into her hands that again smelled of some kind of washing-up liquid or something.

"If I weren't an opera singer, I'd want to be a pianist. A pianist in the ballet department of Ljubljana's high school for the performing arts. I would have three children, a charming husband, a new car every two years, a house by the sea . . ."

"Are you being serious?"

"No, I'm not. But who knows how things would have turned out if I had not had a fight with Ingrid on my twenty-second birthday. If she had not locked me in my room. If I had not thrown my things into a suitcase. If I had not jumped on the first train to Paris . . . If I had not found Madame Kudelka, and so on . . . And who knows where you would be if you weren't here with me."

"I know where I would be. By the sea. I would be walking

along the beach in yellow rubber boots, looking for shells."

"Do you regret not being by the sea, walking along the beach?"

"Let me think about that," I said, and blew into her hands again.

37

Now I can answer your question about the headscarf. The headscarf was a source of great concern in those days before her New Year's Eve concert. When I opened my eyes on one of those mornings, she was again sitting next to me on my bed. The first thing I saw was that headscarf. Those birds of every colour on a sandy background. The knot beneath her chin. The long silk ends hovering above me.

"How innocently you sleep," she said.

Innocently, I repeated in my mind, which is slower in the morning, as I gazed at her. She had already washed and dressed, though she did not look particularly fresh. It must be quite late already, I thought. I am sure it's quite late – I have no trouble sleeping till noon and beyond.

"Lying stock-still," she continued.

I raised myself on my elbows and continued gathering my thoughts.

"Like a child," she added.

A child? I looked at her again. Suddenly, who knows why, I raised myself up towards her and pulled at one of the two ends of her scarf, which unravelled and fell into my hand.

"Why do you wear this?"

She clapped her hand onto her ear. She sat there for a while. Then she snatched the scarf out of my hand, got up, and left the room.

I followed her. The flat was old and large, with high ceilings and a long corridor onto which three rooms opened. And a balcony that ran the length of the flat and looked out on an inner courtyard. The bathroom was also large, with black-and-white ceramic tiles like a chessboard, an old-fashioned washbasin, and a tub with lion's paws. Along the corridor hung lifeless oil portraits that stared at me apathetically. I heard her speaking on the phone in flawless Italian. Probably with Signora Poiatti, her agent, who called her around ten every morning. When she hung up I went into the kitchen. She was sitting with her back to me at our table with the green stems. I saw that she had tied the scarf over her head again. I sat down opposite her, so I could see her face.

"Why do you wear that?" I asked her again.

"Is this another interview?" She looked at me sourly.

"Just this one question."

There was silence. I leaned my head on my hands, as she was doing.

"Because I can hear my heart beating in my ears," she finally said.

Because I can hear my heart beating in my ears, I repeated to myself. Did I understand her correctly? She can hear her heart beating in her ears? I was about to ask her what she meant, when she got up and left the kitchen.

That evening we went to the Ristorante Verdi. We dressed

stylishly: she in elegant boots, a tight skirt, and an orange V-neck pullover, I in a blue velvet shirt and brown trousers. We walked down the stairs together. It was snowing outside. I offered to go back for an umbrella. No, no, she said. She buttoned her brown coat all the way and tightened the knot of her scarf. It was snowing heavily, the flakes melting on our shoulders. We can take the tram, I suggested. No, no, she said again, shaking her head. So we set out on one of our long walks, straight ahead, straight ahead, in Milan we always walked straight ahead. I began to feel cold, the snow was blowing into my eyes and trickling down my neck, and I was wearing the wrong shoes for this weather. But Lea Kralj paid no attention to such trifles. Among prima donnas, Lea Kralj probably had the most stamina and resilience, regardless of Toronto's views on the subject: Exhausted by a taxing opera season, squeezed dry like a lemon, it's not surprising that things went the way they did, is it? Lea Kralj could easily walk kilometre after kilometre without feeling particularly tired or being at all worried about her voice. Quite the opposite. Lea Kralj was a champion, a long-jumper.

By the time we reached the Piazza Mirabello, it had not been snowing for quite a while. Lejka's cheeks were red, and my nose was dripping. The Verdi was full. We were surrounded mainly by couples, needless to say heterosexual couples. Only at one corner table sat two young, carefully dressed men. We were also a couple; not a heterosexual one, nor a homosexual one either, but we were a couple, flashed through my mind. We were approached by a short-necked Italian dressed in black, with slicked-back hair. He greeted us with a short-necked bow, *Signora, Signore,* particularly Lejka, as if he had suddenly recognised her, *Signorina,* of course, *Signorina la cantatrice!* With the trace of a smile he followed her obsequiously, and offered to take her coat to the cloakroom.

"I'll take it," I jumped in. I stepped in front of her and waited for her to take it off and give it to me.

"You've forgotten something," I said softly but firmly, and nodded at her headscarf.

She looked at me as if she wasn't sure what I meant. Then she came closer, until we were only separated by her coat, which I was holding with increasing awkwardness. Then I saw that she *had* understood. She ran her hand over her headscarf and looked away as if it had nothing to do with her, and even less with me. Our Italian came closer so he wouldn't miss the curious scene.

"I haven't forgotten anything," she said coolly. She walked past me and the Italian and headed towards one of the empty tables by the window that had evidently been reserved for us. The Italian and I watched her: I, looking more and more ridiculous as I stood there holding her coat, and the Italian struggling to maintain the grave air of a maître d'hôtel. He and I watched her sit down, lean her elbows on the table, and rub her hands together. Then she settled down and sat staring in front of her. Needless to say, she was the only person in the entire restaurant sitting so motionless, looking straight ahead, the scarf with the colourful birds on her head. I think it was at that moment that I realised for the first time something was wrong.

38

Rubin, and also the Christmas tree, could apply to your question about those little things in which we all recognise ourselves and which are part of our daily routine.

Rubin was a dog that used to lie on the pavement in front of 8 Via Fiori Oscuri. To me he looked like a wolf, though I had never actually seen a real wolf up close. I must describe him, I still remember him as well as if he were lying in front of my door here in the rue Gustave-Doré. A lean, medium-sized animal with fur that was whitish grey and black. (His stomach whitish grey, his back increasingly dark, his head almost black.) Pointed ears and incredible eyes: cold, clear, rimmed with blue as if they were framed. Whenever I walked past the launderette in the Via Fiori Oscuri, I saw him sitting or lying on the pavement by the entrance of number 8. I avoided him more often than not, even stepping off the pavement and then looking back at him. Who did the dog belong to? Dog? He was a cold-eyed wolf! What was he doing in the street all day?

In Milan, Lea Kralj collected the little chocolates that were always served with coffee. Whenever she could, she would snatch my chocolate from under my nose and slip it into her coat pocket along with hers, whispering that it was for Rubin. Probably for the pianist with whom she's preparing her recital, I said to myself, or for some stage-hand. "Oh no, a wolf!" I gasped, when she and I had walked past 8 Via Fiori Oscuri for the first time. Lejka had gone over to him, crouched down, her coat sweeping the wet pavement, and began patting his head. Rubin, Rubinček . . . she said, and other things I didn't understand. She was obviously saying something to him in Slovene and patting him above his cold eyes. The dog stretched his head towards her and she continued uttering the unfamiliar words. Then she unwrapped the little chocolates one by one, and in a flash they disappeared into his jaws. She patted him on the head and the back, got up, and joined me again.

"How do you know his name is Rubin?" I asked, as we walked on.

"I just know," she said. And that was that.

Later I saw her a few more times with Rubin – the last time, she didn't know that I was watching her. She was bending over him so that the ends of her headscarf touched him. From a distance it looked as if she was whispering something in his ear, as if she were telling him something, particularly as the dog was lifting his head to her. She remained above him like that for a long time, so that some passers-by even stopped to look at them.

In and around Sežana, I was to see her patting this or that dog. But none like Rubin, the young wolf.

39

It was the day after our dinner at the Ristorante Verdi (if I am not mistaken), that we finally decorated the Christmas tree. We bought paper of different colours. We sat on the floor. I cut out various shapes – stars, moons, comets, a sun with rays – Lejka pierced them with a needle and a long thread, and strung them over the tree. At first we were so immersed in our work that we barely exchanged a word. Then, as our hands grew more skilful and experienced, doing the work on their own, we began to talk.

"What do you want for a New Year's present?" she asked, looking at me from above as she hung silver moons on the highest branches. "Let's say that I am the Golden Fish and can grant you a wish, a single wish."

"The Golden Fish?"

"Forget the fish – a good fairy."

"I'll have to think about that," I said, continuing to cut out the rays.

"No, no." She shook her pony-tail. "No thinking! These are the kind of wishes one has to have prepared in advance."

She sat down beside me again and picked up the needle and thread. I finished cutting out the last two rays and put down the scissors. Our tree with its celestial bodies was only missing its crown, and perhaps a star or two. Actually, I did have a wish ready. It has been deep in my heart for a long time, I thought as I looked at her hands.

"Well?" She turned towards me and looked at my hands.

"I would like to fall in love, to meet someone who resembles both Pablo and Haas. Who would have Pablo's sinewy body and Haas's arms with their golden hairs, Pablo's independent spirit and Haas's readiness for anything . . . Shall I go on?"

She nodded.

"I'd like to see that man in front of me, suddenly, and know that he's the one. That's it. That's all. What about you?"

She took the sun with the six rays that I was holding and got up. As she secured it at the head of our galaxy she said, "I wish that my mother was already here, and that tonight was New Year's Eve."

40

If I could do it again, I would change my wish. I would wish for something different. Anything. For instance, that Lea Kralj and I had lived together longer, not necessarily in Milan, but as we did in the flat on the Via Fiori Chiari. We were never to live under the same roof again. I mean alone, each with our own concerns, thoughts, sex life, but going for walks together, breakfasting together, shopping together . . . as we used to in the Via Fiori Chiari before it became the Via Fiori Oscuri. I would wish for a new bicycle. A new column in *Petronius*, and with carte blanche, *Monsieur le directeur*! And now that we're on the subject, a new *directeur* too. A Mont Blanc pen from 1935. The ring with the square emerald that I saw at the flea market and which I would have kept in my trouser pocket. Some *fleurs d'oranger* scent. I would wish that the rue du Faubourg Saint-Honoré and the rue Saint-Honoré were closed to cars so I could zigzag down them on my bicycle while gazing at the morning sky and the up-to-the-minute news on the giant screen, the wind chafing my face, ruffling my hair, and making my shirt billow out. I would wish for an unlimited pass to the health club at the Ritz with its swimming pool and *hammam* steam bath. That they would open the

Rijksmuseum in Amsterdam for me alone, and that I could stand as long as I wanted in front of Rembrandt's *Jewish Bride*. Or even wish for impossible things, such as that Divino would relocate itself to a Paris street so that I could continue going there, leaning against the shelves, the evening sun pressing against my back, and that I would still know by heart where to find *Anna Karenina* and *Wild Palms*, but also *American Pastoral* and *Full Moon* and *The Great Gatsby*. Or that my Aunt Anna was still living a few streets away and I could go there for lunch twice a week as I used to, and watch her sitting at her sewing machine or cutting a new pattern. I would wish that I had enough tears and didn't have to wear glasses . . . That I could go to bed earlier . . . That I too could sing . . . I would wish for anything, except for Julijan Remek.

And I would also tell Lea Kralj to change her wish, to forget Madame Ingrid, and to tell herself that New Year's Eve is just an evening like any other.

41

Two days before her mother's expected arrival, when everything was ready for her, when the Christmas tree looked like a whimsical solar system, Madame Ingrid called to say that she wasn't coming to Milan. All Lea Kralj told me was that she wasn't coming. When I returned in the afternoon from enjoying some Milan chic and making a few humdrum purchases, I found her sitting in the kitchen. She was leaning with folded arms on the table and staring straight in front of her. I hadn't expected to find her at home, especially not at that hour. I opened the fridge and put the things I had bought inside. I poured some water into a vase and placed the bouquet in it that the unknown admirer had, as usual, left on the doormat. Then I put the vase on the table and sat down opposite her. I liked the daily ritual of white flowers on the doormat. How wonderful, how elegant those few white flowers were, every day different, lilies, tulips, roses, even garlic blossoms! I was proud of them, as if I had somehow deserved them.

"Here's another bouquet," I said with satisfaction.

It was only then that I actually looked at her. She was ready, I mean: ready, as if she were either waiting for someone or about to leave. Her hair combed. And she was heavily made up, which was unusual for her and markedly changed her face, making it more even and stern. And cold, so that I was almost frightened, as if she was asking herself: What the hell is this man doing in my kitchen, who told him to open and close the fridge, to put the flowers in a vase, my flowers . . . What does he want from me, why is he here in this flat with me? And why does he have that stupid look on his face?

"I have a rehearsal this afternoon and evening, you needn't wait for me," she said finally, unfolding her arms.

I nodded, and rearranged the flowers in the vase. "Don't forget to dress warmly. It's getting colder outside, cold to the bone, real winter, who'd have thought."

"That's great!" She suddenly got up abruptly and went towards the door. "Really great! The colder the better!" At the door she turned and said: "Ingrid phoned to say she won't be coming. *Ciao bello.*"

I heard her lock the front door. I opened the window and waited for her to appear on the street. I saw her heavy coat and the headscarf with the birds. She was walking with long, hard strides, at least that is how it seemed from my standpoint. And she was also in a hurry. Then she suddenly stopped and crouched down. "What's going on?" I wondered. "What's she doing on the ground, the flaps of her coat lying on the muddy snow?" It was only then that I saw Rubin. I saw her pat his head, saw the wolf raise his head meekly towards her. Saw her bend over him, the ends of her headscarf dangling before his eyes. It even seemed to me as if she was telling him something. That she was telling him what she hadn't told me, and that Rubin was listening to her with his blue-rimmed eyes.

42

The day of the New Year's Eve concert was our longest day. Lea Kralj had left in the morning. A car and driver were waiting for her outside. *Ciao bello*, she called at the door as if she were going shopping, and not to a concert. In an instant the flat became so quiet that I could hear myself breathing. The lights on the Christmas tree were blinking silently.

I paced up and down the long hall. Our kitchen hadn't been this empty for quite a while. The dishes were washed. The bouquet of white flowers stood alone on the table. I opened the door to her room, looked at her pyjamas and thick socks lying on the made-up bed. Then I went into the bathroom, which was still damp and warm. I sat down on the edge of the tub with the lion paws. I tried to sing. Just to hear if it really does sound different in the bathroom. I thought perhaps it sounded different. It definitely did sound different, otherwise why would she sing there every morning, and I began to look at the objects around me. Her creams were arranged along the shelf above the radiator. Next to them lay her toothbrush, still wet, and her red toothpaste (Elmex). A comb, a brush, some make-up . . . a bottle of perfume (no brand name). A box of aspirin, Slovenian ones, and contraceptive pills, I think. Her towelling dressing-gown hung on the door. Everything was impeccable, everything in its place, Lea Kralj was the most impossibly clean woman I ever knew. If anything fell on the floor, crumbs for instance, she would immediately sweep them up. If my shoes lay too far apart in the hall, she would automatically put them next to each other as she walked past. She would dry a glass for so long that it was hard to believe there was any glass left in it. The kitchen was always immaculate. And the bathroom, the bathroom smelled of . . . her, of course, and a little bit of me too, and of bleach.

It is not really for me to say whether Lea Kralj sang better than all the others, whether she outshone the other singers at the concert, whether she was the "Queen of the New Year's Eve concert", as you wrote. If you ask Toronto, he will not tell you that he was astounded, that she took his breath away, that he thought he was dreaming, that this was all an illusion, a mirage, two images that for an instant, as if in fun, had merged into one and then after a second or two were no more. Firstly, because he wasn't at the concert and had only, like everyone else, bought the CD. And secondly, had he been at the concert, he would have seen her through different eyes. He and I always saw her through different eyes.

I was sitting in the second row. I had been waiting all day for that moment. I had tried to make the time go faster or slower, to make Milan's geography go into a skid, looking for streets where I knew they weren't, just to do something so that I would suddenly be in a hurry, so that suddenly things would get serious. And finally the moment came. I was sitting in the second row of the concert hall, pleasantly immersed in the hubbub of anticipation around me, in the confusion of perfumes and the bustling of evening gowns. I closed my eyes and waited.

Lea Kralj came after a Swedish baritone. And when it arrived, the moment, I mean, when things finally got serious, everything turned out differently. I told myself that this wasn't real, that I was dreaming, that this was all an illusion, a mirage, two images that for an instant, as if in fun, had merged into one and then after a second or two were no more. She stood, so to speak, in front of me, some thirty or more feet away, slightly elevated – what I mean is, I couldn't look at her face to face, but looked up slightly from below. She was wearing the silky velvet orange dress that the two of us had chosen, cut extremely low, with thin straps that were slanted at an angle, and on her head, on her head she wore the scarf with the birds on a sandy background. The ends hung down to her breasts. When she bowed, the ends swung before her eyes. The hall fell silent in surprise and disbelief. My neighbour leaned over to her neighbour, whispered something in his ear, and tittered.

I closed my eyes, felt the blood pulsating against my

temples. Then I heard the first sounds of the orchestra. And then I heard her voice, nothing out of the ordinary, a clean, smooth, powerful stream pouring into the hall and directly into me (as Lluis Toronto would say, and he would probably add that nobody knows how to pour out Villa-Lobos as she did, to immerse herself in it). Perhaps this was only an illusion, I said to myself one last time, a mirage, two images that for an instant, as if in fun, had merged into one, but which when I would open my eyes would no longer be there. And when I did open them, my eyes suddenly clouded.

It was not an illusion, or a mirage, or a joke . . . She was still standing in the same place in her new orange dress and her old scarf with the colourful birds on her head. Two slanted beams of coloured light were falling on her face: the first – warm, amber, like a golden winter sun – lit and softened her face; the second, a cold blue, framed her as if she were standing before a piece of sky. I could express these things differently, with more distance and aplomb, but I will not. I will only say that this was the most beautiful and touching image of a woman I had ever seen, that I felt a tightening in my pubic region, and that for a few long moments my heart did not know whether it should constrict with sadness or expand with happiness.

43

Petronius Arbiter is an excellent magazine. Deeply superficial, self-absorbed as cashmere, incisive as the best Bordeaux. Directed at the widest range of readers, handling them all with equal unscrupulousness, even contempt (men's shoes with pompoms, or tennis socks off the tennis court, too much jewellery, ties that are too long, or just ties . . . these are details fatal at all levels of society, and *Petronius Arbiter*, notwithstanding the elitism of its taste, is surprisingly democratic, even revolutionary). A magazine open to the widest variety of influences, capable of shedding light in unexpected places (Lea Kralj in Madrid, for instance). Usually swimming against the tide (a tendency for which I am officially responsible, as you can see from the name of my column, *À rebours*, "Against the Grain"). Sexually incorrect (one of the clichés, or hard to prove premises, of our editorial office is that individuals with same-sex orientation are aesthetically more creative). Pessimistic (beauty is not an expression of pleasure, but connected more or less with spleen or with a barely visible veil of sadness, as an Italian aesthete might put it). A recommendable magazine – I actually intended to start with this – above all during times of stress (after all there is nothing more elegant than knowing how to hide one's sadness).

44

It wasn't until the following summer that I met Madame Ingrid. I imagined her to be tall, at least five foot ten, straight-backed, with blond hair that was white at the roots, and with her daughter's long arms, legs, and large feet. A stern woman with hair pulled back into a tight bun at the nape of her neck, lips chapped by wind and clean air and redolent of Vaseline, dressed in circumspect trousers, a man's white dress shirt, and a dark-blue jumper. A retired anaesthesiologist with obsessively clean hands, short nails, and rather good skin for her age. A Slovenian woman with a touch of the Scandinavian about her. I always imagine people before I meet them (or, I should say, I cannot stop myself from imagining them).

She was small. She had short, messy hair that was dyed black and kept falling into her eyes. From time to time she tried flicking it out of the way with her index and middle fingers, between which she was holding a cigarette. The unhealthy skin of a smoker. Lips heavily rouged. A wide, regular, harmonious face, with a large mouth and strong chin. A face that might have been beautiful once, rousing admiration or even uneasiness because of its regularity and harmony, but which had softened with age, lost its precision. Nimble fingers with long nails and countless rings. Movements that were just as nimble and decisive, as if her body knew beforehand every centimetre of space into which she would step or through which she would wave her hand. She was wearing a loose dress that almost reached down to her ankles, nonchalantly erasing the shape of her body. From time to time she adjusted her dress with both hands at the shoulders, only to let it hang down her body again, as if to accentuate the dress's comfort and practicality. Her voice bore a marked resemblance to her daughter's, high and softly hoarse, though in Ingrid's case probably because of her smoking. When she saw me enter the somewhat longish living room in Sežana, she did not get up right away. She looked at me from where she was sitting, slowly put on her glasses, and smiled. Only then did she come towards the door, take my hand in both of hers, and smile at me again.

So that's her, I thought, as she squeezed my wrists, her face bathed in a welcoming smile. Madame Ingrid. Ingrid Kralj, Lejka's mother. The woman who had called Lea one morning in Madrid, and in the twinkling of an eye reduced her to tears. The woman her daughter and I had waited for so ardently in Milan, for whom we had cleaned a flat that wasn't even ours . . . Had bought all kinds of things, even a brand-new Christmas tree which we had decorated – God, how we had decorated it! And then she didn't come. Just like that. Didn't come to the spotless flat, didn't stand beneath the decorated tree. Didn't come to the New Year's Eve concert. Didn't sit in the audience, and didn't catch her breath when her daughter stepped onto the stage. Didn't ask herself: My God, what is she doing wearing that headscarf on stage, in a concert of all places? Didn't rub her eyes to assure herself she wasn't seeing things. Just as later she didn't come into the dressing room. Didn't hug Lejka tightly and ask, "What's wrong, my child?"

If I had to describe Ingrid in a single word, I would say "harmless". Madame Ingrid struck me as charmingly harmless. Even though I know that that doesn't mean a thing to me. Relationships between people are not like chemical elements, compatible or incompatible. Relationships between people are incomprehensible.

45

No, never. July, 1998, was my first time. At last, I said to myself, at last I will see her Slovenia! At last I will understand what it means to live in such a small country and be proud of it. I felt I was getting ready for the most important journey of my life. Even before I reached Slovenia (or rather crossed its border illegally), I fell in love with it. Even after everything that was to happen later, I can still say with conviction that I fell in love with this little country – with its alluring body, its intricate soul – even if later I would also come to hate it.

It all began on the day I met Madame Ingrid for the first time. It was in the morning at the train station in Trieste. The train was coiling in a final wide loop before reaching the terminus, and I leaned my elbows on the window that looked out onto the sea and the sky, and pushed it all the way down. It was summer outside, high summer. And in the midst of that high summer – the sky was a deep blue and the sea rippled silver before my eyes – Lea Kralj was waiting for me in her Slovenia. "Come," she had scribbled in tiny letters, "come at all costs. L. P.S. I have something for you, and I want to show you everything." "Everything" was underlined. Haas, who had almost forgotten about her, began calling her "the Slovenian" again. "What does she mean by 'at all costs'?" he asked me. "And what does she have for you?"

I took off my glasses and let the wind beat my face and ruffle my hair. There was something solemn, even sacrificial, in the air. As if beyond the deep bay and in the midst of that high summer something crucial, even final would take place. I grimaced. All I need, I thought, is a little intense blue and a clear horizon for my thoughts to take a dramatic turn. And I leaned even further out the window, the wind beating down on me even more relentlessly.

By the time the train stopped and I heard the loudspeaker announce "*Trieste, stazione di Trieste, ultima fermata,*" my head was spinning and there was a ringing in my ears. I sat down in my seat and waited for the coach to empty out gradually and for the debris to clear from my head. I caught sight of them when I least expected it. Suddenly they were standing beneath the window from which I had leaned just a little while ago to gaze at the sea. Lea Kralj, lightly tanned and dressed in white: a white T-shirt, tight white trousers, and even a greyish-white checked headscarf, from beneath which peered a lock of blond hair. And he, he stood one step behind her, as if he were not necessarily with her. In an instant I saw that he was the one. He had Pablo's broad forehead and vigilant eyes. Full lips. Blond hair and blond hairs like Lieutenant-Colonel Haas. A touch of nonchalance in the way he carried himself, in his confident walk, in the way he kept his hands in his pockets and the way he glanced at me coolly with narrowed eyes. He, too, was dressed in white: trainers, shorts, and a baggy T-shirt. I sat there smiling at them, the way one smiles at one's destiny.

"What are you waiting for?" Lejka called out.

When I finally got off the train and felt the ground beneath my feet, she flew into my arms.

"*Ciao bello,*" she whispered into my ear. "You see? Just as I promised!"

From the first hug I felt that something in her had changed. She must be in love, I thought. Yes, she's definitely in love. She had a different scent. Her skin was supple and elastic. Her body, too, was supple and elastic, pleasantly relaxed, as after a long period of physical exertion or an orgasm. She took a step back, and I looked at her from head to toe.

"It's because of the wind, the strong Boras," she said, running her hand over her headscarf. Suddenly she untied it and stuffed it into my pocket.

She bit her lip, as if she were trying to stop her mouth from breaking into a smile. Her hair hung almost to her shoulders and kept falling into her eyes, which I could swear were almost as blue as the sky over the bay of Trieste had been just a few moments ago.

Then she turned to him and spoke a long sentence that I obviously did not understand.

"This is my winner, my champion," she said, turning back to me.

"Your champion?" I said, puzzled.

"A real one."

"What do you mean?"

"He's the European archery champion."

"Archery?" I repeated like a fool.

"Bow . . . arrow . . . target," Lejka said, looking first at him, then at me.

As if by a secret signal, he and I simultaneously took a step towards one another, and, reaching out, shook hands.

46

Yes, it's her favourite photograph. Definitely. Under it you will usually see written: "Summer, 1998, Slovenia, private collection." Lea Kralj in the rear-view mirror of her Toyota, with tousled hair, her hand on her forehead sweeping a lock out of her eyes, the two pretty dimples on her cheeks, and a smile about to spread over her lips. Lea Kralj at the wheel, on the windy morning we crossed the Slovenian border illegally. I took the picture.

"Have you ever met an archery star before?" she had asked me with that hidden smile seen in the photograph, as she tried to catch my eye in the rear-view mirror.

"No, no."

"Never?"

"Never."

"That's what I thought."

"What?" I asked.

"That Remek would be your first . . . That's his name, Remek. Julijan Remek. Everyone calls him Julijan. I call him Remek . . . 'R', careful with the 'r'. Roll the 'r' like a grinding mill. In front – between your teeth – not in the back of your throat. And the stress is on the first syllable . . . *Re*-mek," she said, looking at me through the mirror.

"*Re*-mek," I repeated carefully, and so spoke his name for the first time.

They both laughed. Lejka said something in Slovene and touched his thigh for an instant. Remek leaned towards the radio and began searching for a station. There were white specks of paint on his hands and arms. He stopped at a guitar piece that was slow and wandering. Then he sat back in the seat and leaned his head against the headrest. Lejka was concentrating on the road.

I sat back too, took off my glasses, closed my eyes, and sighed. I suddenly felt at ease with the two of them, very much at ease. In her light-green Toyota. On that winding border road. With the slow, let's say, Andalusian guitar. With the occasional Slovene sentence. With the howling wind hurling itself at the trees. And above all, being just a few centimetres from their backs. How long would I be prepared to ride with them this way, I asked myself. As long as possible, was my reply.

Suddenly the Toyota slowed down.

"Open your eyes," Lejka said. "I would like to introduce you to Slovenia."

"Slovenia?" I said, taken aback.

Remek glanced at me over his shoulder. I sat up and leaned my elbows on the backs of their seats, almost touching them.

So this is their Slovenia, I said to myself. That road winding so pleasantly before us, first one way, then the other. All that green, so much green everywhere. That opulent light all around us. Those valleys, the rocks piled high, the tall vines. The pine forests, and still the winding road that grows narrower, straightens out, becomes like a long breath of air. Today perhaps I would say: "Who cares. So there's a lot of green. So there's a patch of sparse pine woodland with a road through it. So there are hills from which you can see valleys, vines, rocks piled high, clustered stone houses ... So it's a winding road. So the wind's blowing. So there's a sign saying: 'Sežana, 18 km'. But back then, on that windy morning in July, sitting a few centimetres from their backs, I fell in love with Slovenia at first sight. With those hills, those valleys, with the colour of the sky, even with the name "Sežana". Whenever I spoke that name, "Sežana" sounded to me as if someone were caressing me, or as if I were caressing someone. (This is why, later, I called the village in which Lejka's house stood "Sežana", even though it had nothing to do with the real Sežana.)

"But we haven't even crossed the border yet," I said, suddenly waking from my stupor.

"Yes we have," Lejka replied. "We took a shortcut. We crossed by a secret place, on the sly, which you can't always do – only when you are with Remek."

"With Remek?"

"The archer. When he's not an archer, he's a customs officer," she said.

47

The house in "Sežana" did not belong to Ingrid, but to her. When Lea Kralj was in Slovenia – less and less in the last few years – she basically lived there. She had been given the house by her Aunt Angela, her father's sister, who had moved with her husband Fabio to the Italian side of the border. While Aunt Angela still had her health she would come once a week to air the house, sweep up, water the garden, particularly the beans and lettuce, and call on her neighbour, Drago, to have a large glass of wine. Then she fell ill, and the house began to smell musty and run down. Her Italian husband went a few times a year, but then that stopped too. One day she telephoned Lejka. Lejka had not seen her for at least fifteen years. Ingrid had cut all ties with her former husband's family and had expected the same of her two daughters. I'd like you to have the house, Aunt Angela had said. So that you have something from your father's sister. God knows it's not worth a lot, and you'll have to make some repairs – it needs a new roof, and the garden needs a lot of work . . . that is, if you want the house, of course, she added, as if she were justifying herself.

That was how one afternoon Lea Kralj ended up with Aunt Angela's house. My house, she had said, trying to accustom herself to her new and only piece of property. First she swept the floors, painted the old furniture, and bought a few pots and pans. Then she began the renovations. First the roof, then the shutters, and then the bathroom, which she had installed in the sunniest spot of the house that looked out over the sea. In the meantime, Aunt Angela died. Then Lea Kralj had it rewired, a new staircase, the kitchen painted. She got rid of the weeds and planted some fruit trees. Whenever she went to the village, she stopped for a glass of wine at the neighbours' the way her aunt had done, particularly old Drago, who lived at the edge of the village. Drago never asked any questions: What kind of prima donna, Angelica, Katya, Tosca? For him she was only the tall woman with the blond pony-tail, an occasional scarf on her head, the woman with hardworking hands who had moved into Angela's house, though she was rarely ever there. He poured her a glass of the dark, violet wine of that region, and watched it stain her lips and teeth. When the house was almost finished, she also had the attic restored, which Ingrid then appropriated in the twinkling of an eye. You can't leave a house standing empty like that, she had said, especially if you are abroad more than you're at home.

The house in Sežana resembled Lea, which I suppose is nothing new. Whether we like it or not, houses and flats end up resembling us. When I first set foot in Lieutenant-Colonel Haas's flat, I saw in an instant whom I was dealing with. The same with Pablo and his square room, the hard futon, the potted aspen and the piles of books. Or with Remek, as I will tell you later. Ingrid's flat in Ljubljana, too, resembled her as one drop of water resembles another. Lea Kralj was no exception. Her house was large and complicated, with its sunny and shadowy sides. It was cheerful, even witty, surprising, open-hearted, from time to time nonchalant, and suddenly, for no obvious reason, incomprehensible, sad, suicidal.

48

Holiday? The concept of taking a holiday was alien to her, though I'm not trying to say that her approach to work was typical of her compatriots. If you asked her what she was up to, she would always reply: "I'm working". But in the Via Fiori Chiari, when I asked her what she intended to do that summer, she told me that she usually turned down all offers for festivals, concerts, recitals and recordings in the summer . . . and that she spent those months at home, mainly with Ingrid. Her agents, old Schimler, and particularly Signorina Poiatti, tore out their hair and called her behaviour unacceptable, even self-destructive. But she maintained that Ingrid was waiting for her, that she was counting on her. "I don't even know what a holiday is," she continued. "Holidays are for people to get away from themselves . . . So that for a while I would no longer have to be me, and you wouldn't have to be you . . . don't you think?" she added.

And yet, during those first days in Sežana there was a wonderful feeling of holiday in the air. We continued driving around in the light-green Toyota. I continued sitting in the back. I continued looking at the countryside around me. And the relentless wind – not wind, Boras, as the two of them corrected me – continued buffeting us.

"Us" meant Lejka, Remek, and I. Lejka was driving (Lejka loved driving), Remek sat next to her, and I sat gazing at them from the back. I, too, was wearing white, even though we were no longer painting her house. We had only painted on the first day after my arrival, or rather we had finished painting the room that the two of them had begun, the upstairs room with the view of the sea. Your room, Lejka had said to me, and she made me move in the following day, even though it still smelled of paint. With our white clothes we looked like a real trio. A trio, not a triangle. That was to come later. "You too?" Ingrid had said when she saw me in the morning in my white shirt and grey trousers. I nodded, without questioning what she might mean.

Not that I asked myself any questions those first few days. I didn't wonder why, for instance, Lea Kralj showed me the house where Remek lived, or the meadow on the village common where he had set up his archery targets. Why she kept driving us around in her car. Nor – and this is the most important thing – why she suddenly played blind on the meadow where the targets stood.

105

"I'm blind," she had suddenly said, and even today I remember the exact place we were standing. We had stopped at the edge of the large meadow, which jutted out abruptly into the valley. There was an aroma of freshly cut grass, even though it had already been raked up. Behind us was a long hedgerow of thorny bushes. In the distance were two undulating hills, and behind one of them, like an elongated triangle, the sea. All this against a very blue backdrop with a still very pale sickle moon, a star or two, and many intense shades of violet on the horizon.

"What?" Remek asked.

"I've lost my sight, I've gone blind," she repeated in Slovene, staring before her with vacant eyes. Remek and I looked at each other. It was in fact the first time he and I really looked at one another. Astonished, curious, but also with something like solidarity and, who knows, perhaps already a touch of betrayal. Remek slid his hands into his pockets and even smiled at me, unless that smile had something to do with Lejka's game. In the meantime, Lejka had taken a few awkward steps, her arms stretched out before her as if she really were blind.

"I don't know what's going on behind my back . . . nor who is who," she called out, and came staggering towards us.

"Who is who?" she repeated in a lower voice, closing her eyes, and zigzagging her way towards Remek. They suddenly stood so close to one another that they could have kissed easily enough, even though Lejka was shorter than him. She reached out and began touching his face. She touched his hair, his forehead, his eyes, and felt her way down to his mouth, running her index finger over his lower lip, slowly

. . . then continuing – running her palm over his neck, his shoulders . . . Remek turned and looked at me. I swallowed nervously, standing a few steps behind them. Her hands continued their journey. Slowly, but in no way shyly or hesitantly. They exuded ownership. I felt my breath chafing my throat, as if something rough were grating in it every time I breathed. I wanted to avert my eyes, turn away, leave them alone. But the more I wanted to retreat, the more I was rooted to the spot. After a few moments, it even seemed to me as if it were my hands travelling down his torso. My hands, stopping for an instant at his waist, as if they wanted to rest or take its measurement. My hands that then made the small detour to his pockets, slipped into them, and touched his wrists.

"But these are *your* hands, Remek!" she exclaimed, as if she were really surprised, pulling them out. Then she turned, pressed her back against him, and folded his arms around her.

"*Ciao bello.*" She looked at me as if she had suddenly woken up and seen me in front of her. I swallowed again. I mustn't forget to tell you that at that moment, leaning against one another in the violet twilight that blurred their features but accentuated their silhouettes, they looked like the most seductive couple I had ever seen. I felt a tightening in my pubic region and closed my eyes.

"Let's go back home," she said, suddenly anxious.

49

On the way home, Lejka and I stopped at one of the roadside inns. The episode I am about to describe is perhaps irrelevant, barely worth mentioning, but when I think back to everything that happened, I feel I simply cannot omit it. What's more, from that evening on everything was to change. The short holiday was to come to an end. Farewell to the drives the three of us had been taking. Farewell to our white work clothes. Farewell to the testing of geographical and other borders.

After our walk in Remek's meadow and Lejka's blind scene, we were all silent for a while, as if something improper had taken place. Lejka and I stopped at one of those inns of the Karst, which even today I don't know whether I like or not. We had dropped Remek off in his village on a hill from which one could see the sea. We ordered two glasses of dark, violet wine and settled down at the counter. In the taproom a few locals were playing cards, with a loud running commentary about the game or God knows what. On top of that, the radio was on – Slovenians are evidently afraid of silence – playing a series of boisterous dance tunes. Lejka was pensive and kept looking at the clock on the wall. I wanted to talk about Remek, where they had met, how things stood between them, and so on. I sipped at the remarkably dark wine that immediately stains your lips, and waited for the radio to switch to music that was a little more *allegro ma non troppo*. Lejka asked if she could use the phone on the other side of the counter.

I watched her pick up the receiver, dial the number, listen, and cover her ear with her free hand. *Halo, Halo,* she called out, as if there was nobody at the other end, or as if she couldn't hear well. I chuckled, wondering why we always raise our voice when we can't hear well. But Lea

Kralj paid no attention to me. Suddenly she turned white, pressed her palm harder against her ear, and almost shouted, *lepo prosim, lepo prosim,* and some other expression that I didn't understand and which she also repeated twice. A few heads turned. Someone even snapped rudely at her. The radio finally took pity on us and went into a *moderato cantabile.*

"*Lepo te prosim,*" she said again, but this time in a quieter, sighing, bitter tone, evidently to herself.

"What's going on?" I asked, walking over to her as she hung up.

"Nothing, nothing at all," she replied with a voiceless laugh.

"What do you mean, 'nothing'?"

"She hung up," she told me with a crooked smile I had never seen on her lips before.

50

Madame Ingrid was evidently one of those mothers who was intent on remaining a mother to the end of her life. By this I mean (and I confess that it strikes me as odd to make this point, since I never really knew my parents, and only rarely called Anna "Mama" – once on a beach in Brittany, for instance, in front of some boys who didn't know that my "Mama" was in fact my aunt) – by this I mean one of those mothers who refuse to accept the law of nature that at a certain point a mother becomes her daughter's daughter. In other words, mothers accepting the fact that at some stage their daughter becomes prettier and cleverer than they, that their daughter's path through life is wider and will take them further. With Ingrid and Lea Kralj all this was also complicated by a form of torture and self-torture, to which people of their country seemed to abandon themselves with particular pleasure. Needless to say, I am writing this now when I know how things were to turn out, having witnessed everything with my own eyes and done nothing to prevent it. But at the time nothing struck me as particularly extraordinary, nor was I really interested in what was going on.

I was interested in Remek. I constantly thought of that first moment when I saw him and Lejka at the station in Trieste, dressed in white and with specks of white paint on their hands, arms, and necks, as if it were some subtle make-up and not spots of whitewash, as I was to realise the next morning. And the days that followed, when I drove about Sežana with them in the light-green Toyota, sitting a few inches from their backs, smelling his scent (Remek smelled of mineral water, no, of a swimming pool, of a lightly chlorinated swimming pool), and that concentration of his (or calm, or indifference, which didn't seem unusual in a champion archer). And Lejka's hands that travelled down his body, his neck, his shoulders, that stopped at his waist as if they wanted to take its measurement, that slipped into his pockets. That slid over his hands in his pockets and pulled them out. And that clasped them, as she folded his arms around her, pressing against him.

I was also interested in Slovenia. I gazed at this country, which I had heard about for the first time in the downstairs area of the Coq Hardi restaurant in Madrid. "Slovenia, do you know it?" she had asked. I no longer remember if I nodded or shook my head.

Now I know it. I know the meadows and the commons and the valleys that surround Sežana. The border crossings to Italy, the legal and the illegal ones. Vines that grow so tall you can walk beneath them. Grottoes and caves and other incredible subterranean phenomena. The patch of sparse pine woodland. The views of the sea, particularly the one from Remek's meadow. The thin blanket of reddish earth over a thick layer of hard stones. Stone walls around the fields, many stone walls. Villages, Lejka's Sežana (which in reality wasn't Sežana), and Remek's village with its ominous name, Temnica, "dungeon". The inns. The dark, violet wine that stains your mouth as if you had eaten blueberries. Lejka's neighbour, Drago, who was pleasant to me as few people were. I know some Slovene words, like the line: *Kaj jo je prignalo, od kod je le prišla čisto noter vate jokat lastovka*. But also Ljubljana, and everything that took place afterwards. And now even this contest for Slovenia's Woman of the Year. (No, not year, century.)

But I did not pay all that much attention to what was going on between Madame Ingrid and Lea Kralj. I could see, of course, that something was. For instance, on the evening we went to that inn and Lejka had begged her on the phone – not begged her, beseeched her – not to hang up, when we came home Madame Ingrid acted as if her daughter were invisible. I could see that Madame Ingrid was speaking only with me, asking where we had been, what I thought of Slovenia, was I hungry, did I want to drink something. If she did turn towards her daughter, who was sitting in an armchair near me, it was merely by chance, the way one's eyes might flit over an empty chair or a spot on the wall. Lejka bit her lip and tried to stay as calm as possible. Her face was no longer the one I had seen a few hours ago on Remek's meadow: playful, sensual, sovereign. It was taut, Baconesque, watchful. Madame Ingrid was obviously pleased.

51

Her everyday life in Sežana and later on did not have anything of the prima donna about it, if that is what you are thinking. Her mother had taken her in hand. Lea has to rest, she told the neighbours and anyone within earshot. She has to have a balanced diet. Get some sleep. Breathe some fresh air but avoid draughts (in Slovenia everyone is afraid of draughts). Go for walks, get some exercise. In short, live healthily and not irregularly – God knows what sort of life she leads all year in those hotels and theatres. And Madame Ingrid knows the meaning of a regular life. She is even prepared to sacrifice her holidays to regulate the life of her elder daughter. Especially as she didn't manage to see her all that much – only from time to time during the year, and luckily during the summer. During the summer Madame Ingrid takes things in hand.

At first I had the impression that this regulated life could be quite pleasant. As Lejka's guest I could also take part in it. This meant a hearty but balanced breakfast on the terrace overlooking the sea. Catching some sun after breakfast. For Lejka, vocalising in the bathroom (which you couldn't hear, as she would let the water run in the bath here too) and studying new roles. Cleaning the house. For me, lazing about and from time to time writing something for *Petronius*. For Ingrid, rummaging around in the attic. Rearranging the plants she was drying. Shopping in the nearest village. Coffee in the nearest village. Lunch, this time in the pleasant coolness of the kitchen. Conversation around the table. An afternoon nap during the hottest part of the day. A walk, picking plants, watering the garden. Some visitors. A light supper. Sitting on the terrace. Herbal tea or a glass or two of dark, violet wine. A light breeze. A clear sky. Millions of stars. And then some time to oneself . . . *Ciao bello*, she would say in lieu of goodnight, and quickly wave her hand.

At times we stayed together for a while in her room. I would lie on the floor, resting my head on my arms, listening to Brahms and watching the effect this regulated life had on her. Had something changed since the Via Fiori Chiari? Did the fresh air, the balanced diet, and the tranquillity show in the glow of her skin? Was she finally calm, even happy? Under her roof, at home, and with Madame Ingrid? Are those closest to us really the people who are closest and most well-disposed, I wondered, glancing at her and then at the ceiling.

Nothing seemed less certain, or what I mean is that I didn't see anything that would have led me to answer any of these questions in the affirmative.

52

It was during those days that I decided to write something about Slovenia for *Petronius*: two and a half typed pages for my column "Against the Grain", I told myself. For during my first days in Sežana, Slovenia had struck me as very much against the grain, and I must stress that in my *Petronius* articles the expression "against the grain" is very positive indeed.

The best example of the positive connotation of this expression was Pablo's bookshop in Madrid, Divino, about which I had also published a piece in *Petronius* a few years back. Divino was a bookshop that could not be more against the grain. Have you ever heard of a bookshop (it was so narrow that two people could barely squeeze past one another between the rows of shelves) that sells only titles from the personal pantheon of its owner? But a vast pantheon, for its shelves brought together novels you would never find side by side anywhere else, except perhaps on R. A. Tibor's shelves. Not to mention the Divino's shop window, where a white opal lamp hung low over a flock of woollen toy sheep and stacks of books, nor the gilded, hand-written shop sign, the pervasive smell (a mix of paper, dried oranges, and nicotine), the two old leather armchairs in which one could lounge all day, the side entrance through which Pablo's women friends would slip in unexpectedly – and not to mention Pablo, who was the most "against the grain" of all.

Slovenia – and especially Sežana and the area around it – struck me as just as unique as Pablo's bookshop. Everything: the harsh rocky landscape, the fertile valleys, the wonderful meadows, the incredible subterranean phenomena, the grottoes with their stalactites and blind fish with human skin, disappearing rivers and even lakes, horses born brown but later turning white, tall vines, and dark, violet wine, customs officers who are also champion archers, and even a few days of regulated living. All this seemed to me irreplaceable, delightful, unique – simply against the grain. Later, particularly in Ljubljana, I would no longer use such words.

53

No, I do not believe she loved nature. Well, not like her compatriots, who head for the mountains en masse, wend their way up to the highest peaks, pick mushrooms, catch trout, and are happy. Nor like the other candidates for Slovenia's Woman of the Century, who are probably all confirmed nature lovers. Nor like her mother Ingrid, who knows every medicinal or poisonous plant. Lea Kralj liked long walks, no matter where: in Madrid at night, in Milan through snowdrifts, in Paris tirelessly along the rue de Rivoli, in Ljubljana desperately up and down the street that used to be called Tito Avenue. The important thing was to walk straight ahead, always straight ahead, to feel the earth beneath one's feet, to let one's thoughts roam free. Like Pablo, Lea Kralj loved trees. She loved looking at them, listening to the wind blowing through them, leaning against their trunks. She loved fruits and vegetables. She helped Drago shell beans. She could spend hours gazing at the vines, the meadows, and the sea beyond them.

But nature itself meant nothing to her . . . that is to say nothing inspiring or cheering – perhaps just the opposite. When Madame Ingrid said – "Let's go out into nature!" – by which she meant going to pick plants – Lejka always agreed, but not because she loved nature.

I went with them a few times, before I started pursuing Remek. I was the observer. The observer of everything. Nature, the landscape, the sky, and the two women in front of me. I was perhaps not the sharpest and most discerning observer, but an observer anyway. When Madame Ingrid pointed at a certain plant, explained its properties, even told us its Latin name, I tried to remember it. *Materina Dušica* – "mother's little soul" – is the Slovene for thyme . . . *Dobra misel* – "good thought" – is oregano . . . *Resje* . . . *Šentžanževka* . . . *robidnice* . . . *pelin* . . . *grenki pelin* . . . careful, the highly poisonous *navadni vratič*, which you'd better know how to use, or turn your back and hurry on.

I remember the places we visited, the valleys we went down into, the meadows we crossed. I remember the colour of the grass (matte gold) and the wild garlic blossoms (light violet). I remember the soft arc of the sky above us. I remember the incredible silence, as if we were alone on the earth except for the insects hidden in the grass and the few birds above us. And of course I remember us, particularly my companions – no, it was I who was the companion – I remember the two women, mother and daughter, who were walking in front of me. Madame Ingrid, in her loose dress and plimsolls, her glasses on her head, her basket and gardening scissors, looking very intent, even solemn. She walked slowly and straight-backed, as if she were keeping an eye on everything, had everything under control. From time to time she would stop, bend down, put on her glasses, and take out her scissors. She snipped off the plant, sniffed it, examined it, and put it in her basket. Then she lit a cigarette and looked at the vista around her. Lejka walked in front of her, without a basket or scissors of course. At times she walked so far ahead that she became smaller and smaller and we could hardly see her. Then she would stop and wait for us to catch up with her. From behind, she looked untroubled, even light-hearted. A red spot (she was wearing a long red skirt) on a pale gold background. When she turned to look back – as if she wanted to assure herself that Ingrid and I were still there – I wondered each time what she was thinking about, why she was walking alone, and if in the end things would turn out the way she wanted.

Today I think that she wanted to leave. That a weak, barely audible voice told her in a whisper that she should speed up her pace and keep walking straight ahead, always straight ahead, not turn back, not at any cost, in life one has to be able to turn one's back and walk straight on ahead, leave things behind, leave, save oneself before it is too late. But when the distance between us grew so wide that we could barely make each other out, when her inner voice became increasingly daring, she suddenly grew frightened, stopped, and waited for us to draw near.

54

"Lejka was a stubborn child. Stubborn, but also obedient. It depended on the situation, of course. I will tell you a little story," Madame Ingrid began for the first and last time. I mean the first and last time she told me anything about her daughter. "When she was three, three and a half, I can't remember exactly, but anyway her younger sister Mili hadn't been born yet and we were still a family, a normal family, we had gone on a bus trip. On the way back, when we were sitting in the bus again, she suddenly began to shout: 'I don't want to go by bus, not by bus, not by bus!' My ex-husband and I tried to reason with her, to make her change her mind, or at least shut up. But Lejka kept shouting, 'Not by bus, not by bus!' Until the driver stopped, turned around to see who was making all the noise, and asked her: 'So how would you like to go, if not by bus?' Lejka stopped shouting as if she had been cut off. Then she stood up between the two rows of seats and shouted: 'By shoes!' The people in the bus burst out laughing, the driver too, and my ex-husband and I had no choice but to get off the bus with her and go back to town on foot. Can you imagine?

"This stubbornness of hers didn't go away with time. I don't know if you are aware of this, but she was a truly talented pianist. Everybody agreed that she had to develop that talent. I too, as you can imagine, tried to encourage her. I paid for the best teacher in Ljubljana. A concert pianist, the very best. But Lea wanted to sing. To sing, and nothing else. When she was ten years old, she knew the whole Mario Del Monaco record by heart. The tenor arias from *Il Trovatore*, *La Traviata*, *Tosca*, and God knows what else. Anyway, when she thought nobody was home, she'd stand in front of the turned-off TV set in the living room and sing, can you imagine?

"Now she sings. Really sings. Though I admit that for a long time nobody believed in her. For years she was just a stand-in. You know what a stand-in is, don't you? A singer who sings in place of the prima donna during rehearsals. All a prima donna has to do is open her mouth wide and wave her arms.

"In other ways she was generally quite obedient. She was a great support when my ex-husband left and I suddenly found myself alone, with her and her sister to raise. Someone had to help me . . . had to stand at my side. She was still small. I don't know if you can imagine what that meant to me. I hope you can. Alone with two little girls and a letter. He only sent one. That he didn't want to live with me any more, but that he would send money for the children. That the girls had nothing to do with this. In a single night my whole life was turned upside down. Lea has never had to go through anything like this. She has no idea what real life is. What it means to be a mother, to be alone with two children, sacrificing oneself for one's children, living for one's children. Lea sings. She roams about the world singing. But what about us?"

55

But what about us? Good point. At times I envied Lea. Not her success, the way Ingrid did (it isn't always easy to accept and rejoice in the success of those nearest to us, don't you think?). I would also not have used Ingrid's words "she roams about the world singing". Ingrid was always comparing herself to her daughter, even when there was nothing to compare. As I see it, beside Lea Kralj's real, everyday world that is like ours, she had another world. Another life. Music, the stage, opera heroines, Angelica, Katya, Tosca . . . Their love, jealousy, anguish, joy . . . Something one sees in writers too, even the worst. Even the worst writers live another life beside their everyday one. The imaginary life of their protagonists, their imaginary world, which can quite easily become more real than their real lives.

Like most people, I only have the one, everyday life: I get up in the morning, I hear the new-born babies crying in the hospital across the street, I sit on the floor with a glass of milk. And in the evenings and at night I find myself again on that same floor – and despite Haas's patience and his readiness for anything, nothing unique ever happens to me.

56

There are of course some things I would prefer to keep to myself. One of the conversations we had in the Via Fiori

Chiari, for instance, which was strictly personal. Some images of her that are firmly embedded within me and that I do not want to share with anyone. Also the story with Julijan Remek. Everything that happened and didn't happen between us. And yet I will most probably never again set out to recount this long journey in quite this way – question after question, step after step: Madrid, Paris, Milan, and now Sežana. And without Remek this journey would not have been what it was. Even today, when the unforgettable storm over Sežana has ebbed in my memory, Remek is still a true mystery to me. Remek could easily come under the heading of the men in her life – her relations with the opposite sex, as you yourself have put it, her emotional and sex life. Yet he could also come under the heading of the relationship between her and me. Whichever way you look at it, Remek came between us. Remek was the archer, I the target, and Lea Kralj the one who placed the arrow in his bow.

If I tell you that he was the most even-keeled man I have ever met, I suppose you would not be surprised: How can a man be a champion archer and also a customs officer if he cannot control his emotions? But something hot also flowed in Remek's veins, something sensual, seductive, a liquid that in a flash could begin to throb in the temples, dulling the eye. That is indeed how it was. Remek's charm, his seductiveness, his sex appeal, as Lea put it, lay in the dual nature of his blood, hot and cold, which one could sense even if one wasn't focusing on him. But I focused on him, from the very first moment.

"So where did you meet him?" I asked her. We were sitting in the kitchen of her house in Sežana. I was sitting and she was leaning with folded arms against the oven, which she had just been cleaning, and I remembered our intimate mornings in the Via Fiori Chiari. Except that in Sežana the sky was blue, and the dull heat was ready to descend upon us at any moment.

"Is this another interview?" she said, laughing and coming closer. She leaned towards me, placed her elbows on the table, and rested her chin on her palm. The word "interview" had gradually taken on a special meaning – something rare, open-hearted, intimate. "The past few days I've been waiting for you to ask me about him."

"Sit down."

"No, no."

"Where did you find Remek?"

"At the border crossing."

"What do you mean 'at the border crossing'?"

"I found him at the border crossing and took him with me. No, he took me with him. To the meadow and then straight to his room in Temnica. A room one does not forget so easily, as you will see."

"Slow down a bit – I'm not following you at all. And sit down, for goodness sake."

She finally sat down and crossed her arms, which again smelled of God knows what cleaning liquid.

"What is it you don't follow? Do I have to paint you a picture?" she asked, leaning even closer to me, and I gazed at the yellowish freckles beneath her eyes and the semi-circular creases near her mouth that I had already come to like in Madrid. But there was also something new and hard that I was seeing for the first time.

"Tell me once more," I said.

57

I am starting a new chapter, though I could just as well have continued with the last one. Lea Kralj and her uncomplicated (believe me!) approach to men. Her ancillary affairs, as I have already called them. Affairs that were quick, hidden, backstage, though at times also right in front of everyone, playful, lasting as long as a siesta. It all depended. If you win, you're mine. Remek was a winner, Remek was a real trophy.

It was at the end of winter, two months after she and I had decorated the Christmas tree in the Via Fiori Chiari. She went for a week to Sežana after recording *Tosca* for a Franco-German television production. She drove through the Karst in her light-green Toyota. She stopped at one of the remote local border crossings. It was the middle of the afternoon, but the sky was already beginning to redden in the west. The air was cold and clean, the trees bare and essential. It was clear that winter was trying to hang on. She rolled down the window and waved her passport. A moment later his face appeared in the frame of the car window. And at that very instant, the instant she set eyes on him – the calm oval of his face, his calm eyes, his full lips and very short, blond hair – she knew that he was the one. When he spoke, she saw his breath in the cold air.

"You cannot cross the border with this registration," he said.

"So what do I need?" she asked, still watching the traces of his breath.

"A different one. A Slovenian one. One from here," he replied.

She looked around, as if she needed a moment or two to think.

"Can I cross with yours?" she suddenly asked, looking into his calm eyes.

Later, when the sky in the west grew increasingly purple, pink, and yellow, though it was still early, and the trees lay like dark patterns against it, the two of them were sitting next to each other in his car.

"What's that bow on the backseat for?" she asked.

Remek, as always, was taciturn.

"I'll show you," he answered softly.

He turned left towards a wooded area. They got out of the car near his meadow. Remek took his bow and arrow. They walked side by side, barely exchanging a word. Lejka looked at his profile, his hard strides, his hands swinging next to her. When they arrived and she saw the targets lined up, she understood right away. He took an arrow, drew the bow, raised it to his ear, and stood stock-still. The arrow hurtled through the air as if to pierce the sun, which was growing redder by the moment.

"Bull's-eye!" she exclaimed.

Later, after the red sun had already disappeared, he opened the door of his room for her. It was large, incredibly large for a bedroom. With freshly painted white walls. A big, old wardrobe that smelled of beeswax. And an equally old double bed that wasn't standing by the wall, but in the middle of the room. Above it – just as in Pablo's room – hung a dim lamp of milky opal. And on the wall facing the bed hung an old colour print of Jesus, of the kind our grandmothers used to have in their bedrooms, she said. "At least I think it's Jesus . . . A man with long hair, a serious smile, and a blue tunic. And with his heart in his hand. His hand is pierced, as if by an arrow. But his heart is untouched, big, red, enveloped in a milky aura . . . The whole thing is quite strange, as you yourself will see," she whispered, and leaned even closer to me. Drops of sweat had gathered around her eyes. I too was beginning to feel hot.

58

When I think about it all today, it was she who sent me to Remek. Of course she didn't actually say: "Aren't you bored being here with Ingrid and me all the time? The days are getting longer and the heat unbearable – take my Toyota and go for a drive. You could drive out to the border. To the meadow with the targets. Or even to Remek's village up on the mountain. You know the way, why don't you?"

But I felt that she was also trying to steer me in the opposite direction: "Stay here with me, only with me. Don't let me out of your sight . . . As you can see, everything's going wrong. Why do you think I asked you to come with me?"

For in the last few days, despite Ingrid's healthy life and harmless smile, something unhealthy and harmful had begun to sprout in the house. Ingrid was again walking about the place as if her daughter were invisible, all the while watching her from the corner of her eye. At times she would speak a few sharp words to her, which I could tell were not a compliment or joke, or anything pleasant. Several times Lejka replied as if she were – God knows why – begging forgiveness for something she had done. She only raised her voice once, but otherwise kept her lips tightly shut, and covered the dark rings beneath her eyes with a layer of make-up. "Mothers and daughters!" I said to myself with a shrug, as if I were an expert. All this had nothing to do with me. It was none of my business. But I noticed that on the afternoon I finally did ask Lea for her Toyota, she had again begun wearing her headscarf with the colourful birds. If there was someone who knew anything about her headscarf, it was me.

"Here's the key," she said, and added, "If you happen to run into Remek, give him my regards."

I turned my head as if I were looking for somebody and had missed her last words.

"OK?" she said, coming towards me, so that I had to look into her eyes.

"OK," I said.

"He told me that he has started training again," she continued, as if she were talking to herself, and began closing the shutters. "There's a new competition soon . . . only a national one, but still . . . even for a national competition you have to be in top shape. What we need more than anything is a good storm. It hasn't been so hot and humid for a long time. After the storm, everything will be different, you'll see," she added.

As I sat at the wheel of her Toyota, speeding down the winding road, I still had her image before me – the image of a tall woman in a red dress and a tight sleeveless blouse, closing the shutters with her long soft arms. Her hair that struck me as always lighter in the morning than in the evening was peering out from under her headscarf. Her eyes that also changed colour. On that day they were a lifeless grey, like the heavy sky. A lifeless grey and ready for anything. Or to put it differently: what will happen will happen.

59

He wasn't at the border. I turned back and drove along the winding road. I no longer saw before me the image of a woman in a red dress and tight blouse looking at me with grey eyes, telling me something I did not want to understand. All I saw was the winding road, the stone walls around the fields, the tall vines, the green valleys . . . I opened both windows, creating a draught that that cooled me down a little. For a few seconds I even stuck my head outside and shouted, yes, shouted . . . Uaaaaa! . . . It immediately vanished in the wind, but it pleasantly emptied my lungs.

I looked for clouds. There wasn't a single one. For a living soul. There wasn't a single one either. I tried to sing something (I, who cannot sing!). *Kaj jo je prignalo, od kod je le prišla* . . . It had never crossed my mind before what a singular delight it must be to be able to sing. To fill one's ribcage with air . . . To control one's breath . . . To feel the tension in one's diaphragm and one's other organs . . . The sound germinating deep within one's inner walls . . . and then to hear it . . . Finally I saw a car driving towards me.

I turned into the road leading to Remek's meadow. I seemed to recall that it was after the second patch of woodland on the left. So after two stretches of road that cut through the sparse pine woods, I turned left. I parked the Toyota at the end of the dirt track that led through the first meadow, and walked downhill between the vines. I crossed the fields and abandoned pastures, looking for openings between the stone walls and thorny hedges. Then I recognised the place. A feminine curve jutting out abruptly into the valley. In the middle of the curve, a broad stretch of flat land with a few trees. In the distance, the two undulating hills, and behind one of them, like an elongated triangle, the sea. Behind me there was a long hedgerow of thorny bushes.

I rolled up my sleeves and made my way to a place where the slope was less steep. The meadow carried me forwards, my legs barely keeping up. I looked around. Nobody anywhere . . . except for invisible insects and birds. I again thought of the seductive forms of this land, of its captivating profile. And I continued towards it, as if I were courting it. Onwards until I get there, I said to myself.

Suddenly a frightening shout came from somewhere, and I froze. Then I heard some fitful movements behind me. I saw a man only a few paces away.

There was another shout: "*Ali si nor?*"

It was Remek, out of breath, his face grey, the veins in

his neck bulging. On his right hand he was wearing a leather strap stretched over his palm, his wrist, and part of his arm. Attached to his belt was a leather quiver. His T-shirt was so tight that I could see his ribcage, now gradually calming down. There was a barely noticeable tremor on his lips.

"*Lahko bi te ubil*," he said.

60

Lahko bi te ubil . . . I still sometimes whisper on the floor of my long and narrow room in the rue Gustave-Doré. "What did you say?" Haas or someone else will ask. *Ali si nor, čisto nor* . . . I smile to myself and walk over to the window. *Lahko bi te ubil* – I could have killed you – and *Ali si nor?* – Are you mad? – are among the few Slovene expressions (along with the couplet about the nightingales and the names of a few medicinal plants) that I still remember and sometimes repeat, as if they were words of savage tenderness.

The following day I learned what they meant. Remek was again wearing a tight blue T-shirt, some kind of thin, baggy trousers, his leather quiver attached at an angle to his belt, and the leather strap over his left hand and arm. His face had regained its healthy colour and his neck its feminine smoothness. In a calm voice and in his faulty customs-officer Italian he told me that he couldn't imagine anyone so reckless as to go for a walk on an archery field. And without looking left or right, as I had done the previous day. Sleepwalking in the broad daylight! What was I looking for? What was I looking at? Didn't I see how dangerous it was? He looked me in the eyes. Dangerous, he repeated.

"I could have killed you," he said again, but this time softly, half to himself, a pensive smile about his lips. Then he went back to his targets and left me alone.

Julijan Remek did not resemble anybody. Let us say that he had Pablo's sinewy body and Haas's long arms with golden hairs. Pablo's walk, his soft elasticity, and Haas's readiness for anything. But I had never met anyone who was so present and so absent at the same time. Someone who in the most offhand manner could simply turn his back and walk away from me, forget all about me, but at the same time give me the feeling that I was not alone.

Who knows how long I sat at the edge of Remek's meadow, where the flat land with its few trees begins. I lay down beneath one of them and watched my handsome archer. Remek did not let himself be distracted. With endless patience – at least that is how I interpreted it – he kept executing the same movements over and over. He placed himself in position, took an arrow, drew his bow, braced himself, took aim, and shot the arrow.

"Do you want to have a go?" he called out to me when I least expected it.

Me? I walked over to him. Even after the hundreds of arrows he had shot, he still smelled of a lightly chlorinated swimming pool. I put my glasses in my pocket. I raised his bow and took an arrow. From a distance it had seemed easy enough to draw the bow to one's face and shoot.

"Not like that," he said, laughing.

He came up behind me and laid his hands on my

shoulders. He waited for my hands to calm down, to forget themselves, which wasn't easy, which you could say was impossible. Then, when they still hadn't forgotten themselves, he – still behind me – steadied the bow with one hand and took hold of my wrist with the other. I felt the touch of his stomach, his chin. His calm breath on my neck. Its warmth. For a moment I thought of Lejka, for a fraction of a second I even saw her, closing the shutters with her long arms, saw her hands travelling down Remek's torso.

"You must think of nothing except that point in front of you . . . And then not even that point . . . Of nothing . . . Absolutely nothing," Remek said, as if he had read my thoughts.

I continued trying. To feel the ground, to brace myself, to calm my breath, to lower my centre of gravity, to the second vertebra, from the bottom upwards as Remek had said, to make the right movement, the one and only right movement, and above all to forget about the three of us, forget about Remek, Lejka, and myself.

61

With every day, Lea Kralj became more and more silent in her house in Sežana. "Silent" meant that she spent half the day in her bathroom, singing, letting the water run, and avoiding me for the rest of the day – unless it was I who was avoiding her – and watching me from a distance. If she did say something, it was usually about the weather, the wind that kept shifting, the humidity that was becoming unbearable, and the storm that already should have come.

"Today the weather will break. Today something will happen," she announced on the day of the storm, and already in the morning began closing the shutters.

"Our meteorologist is never wrong," Madame Ingrid said behind her with a malicious smile.

Lejka continued closing the shutters as if she hadn't heard.

"When things break loose here, they really break loose," she whispered to me.

When I reached Remek's meadow, the sky was still a tedious blue and without the smallest cloud. Remek paid no attention to me, even though he saw me sit down as I had done before between the two trees. As on the previous day, he kept unflinchingly executing the same movements. When the bull's-eye of his target was full, he put down his bow and went over to gather the arrows. Then he started again. And again. One had the feeling that for him time flowed differently.

"Come over here," he called out to me.

"He wants me to have a try this late in the day?" I thought to myself, looking around as I walked towards him. Remek also looked around, and muttered something.

"Yes?" I said.

He nodded towards the darkening sky above us and handed me his bow. "Are you ready?"

I told him I was, and stood in his place. The bow no longer fell from my hands, and the arrow was light as a feather. I was about to draw the bow when a bolt of lightning split the sky in two before me. A few seconds later there was thunder behind the hills on either side of the valley. The storm, flashed through my mind. When things break loose here, they really break loose, I heard Lejka's voice. The wind surged in the nearby trees.

"There's nothing to worry about," Remek said. "Ready?"

I nodded, though I wasn't sure what he meant. He came up behind me and laughed.

"Now that we've begun . . ." I heard him say in the surging of the wind.

"Now that we've begun . . ." I repeated, as if I were his mirror image.

I raised the bow. Drew the string all the way to my face. Held it with all my might. Took aim. The wind in the trees was becoming louder. Remek moved closer to my shoulders. As close as if he were drawing the bow.

"Go on! Shoot! What are you waiting for?" I heard him say in the rising storm.

Not yet, I said to myself, not yet.

"What are you waiting for?" he shouted again, coming even closer.

Not yet, not yet.

"Go on!"

Just as the arrow shot through the air, the clouds burst.

62

If I could do it again, I would not change a thing in that long stormy night. Or rather: has someone already stopped the storm, re-established the electricity, and stopped the morning from tearing itself from the night?

I would again shoot my arrow just as I had done: in the sudden darkening of the sky, the wind rising from God knows where and surging in the trees, with Remek so close behind me that I could barely tell his breath from mine. He would once again laugh at the idea of shooting an arrow with a storm rising . . . who had ever heard of such a thing . . . I would even go and look for the arrow – after all, I wanted to see where it had struck. And Remek, who had gathered up all his equipment and was running along the ridge, would certainly again shout after me: *Kaj si nor, čisto nor* . . .

And then I would run after him, laughing, calling out to him: *nor čisto nor čisto nor čisto nor* . . . Then we would reach Lejka's Toyota, wet and out of breath, the storm raging, and me still laughing . . . *norčistonorčistonor* . . . The trees would bend more and more in the wind, and the path between the vines would become a torrent growing with every minute . . . Give me the keys, Remek would shout, deciding to take matters in his own hands.

We would jump into the Toyota and begin taking off our wet tennis shoes, our T-shirts . . . Suddenly I would become serious, even worried . . . The sky would split open before our eyes as if it were going to break in two . . . I had never seen anything like it . . . Luckily Remek would remain calm . . . He would switch on the engine and the lights, and roll along the top of the hill . . . slowly . . . somehow . . . even though we couldn't see a thing in front of us . . . And the rain would continue pouring down in buckets on the poor Toyota . . .

When we would reach the asphalt road with great difficulty, we would again take the road leading to Remek's
village. Where else could we go? We would continue driving
in silence, feeling alone in the midst of the universal uproar
. . . When we would finally arrive in Remek's courtyard, we
would remain for a while in the Toyota. Let's run for it,
Remek would say. Barefoot and bare-chested, we would
race through the courtyard. Remek would turn on the lights
in the house and climb the stairs to the upper floor.

When we would enter his room and Remek would close
the door behind him, we would breathe a sigh of relief and
glance at one another. This time it would be Remek who
would laugh. We would be dripping wet. "Use this"—he
would throw me a towel and would begin towelling himself
down too. Face, hair, shoulders, chest, armpits . . . I would
look around the room . . .

I would remember Lejka's words: Large, incredibly large
for a bedroom . . . with freshly painted, white walls . . . a
big, old wardrobe . . . and an equally old double bed
standing in the middle of the room . . . and on the wall in
front of the bed, a colour print . . . Jesus . . . pierced hand
. . . red heart . . . and when my eyes groped their way to
that red heart, when I walked a few steps towards it, really,
what a heart, as if it were beating, as if it were alive, the
light would suddenly go out. "Where are you going?"
Remek would ask. "Nowhere," I would reply, though I
could just as easily have said: "To the heart." Or something
of the sort . . . "There's a power cut," Remek would say.
We would continue standing there for a while. What were
we waiting for? "We'd better go to bed," Remek would

continue. I would imagine him taking off his trousers . . . When the lightning lit up the room, I saw his wonderful *ricardo* . . . Then I would hear him climbing into bed, and the bed sighing beneath him.

"Well, what are you waiting for?" he would say.

"Yes, what am I waiting for?" I would echo.

I would climb into bed, lie down, and pull the covers over the head of my troubled *ricardo* . . . And the storm would continue raging . . . It would continue lighting up the night and beating against the large bedroom without respite . . .

"This is incredible," I would whisper

"Shh," he would say.

63

The morning that followed was definitely the most unforgettable of all the mornings Lea and I had spent together. When I opened my eyes she was sitting in front of me. My eyes smarted and my head was burning. Every corner of the room was filled with blinding light. Outside, insects hummed and birds twittered. There was something clean, fresh, and new-born in the air. Even wondrous. If the long ends of her scarf had not been dangling above me, I would have thought that Lea Kralj was an apparition, a colour print like Jesus with his heart in his hand. "My God, what is she doing here?" I thought. "How did she get here? Am I even awake? Was there really a storm last night? Was it just a dream?"

"How innocently you sleep," she whispered.

Innocently, I repeated to myself, and continued to look at her without moving. All of a sudden I remembered another similar moment, not sunny and fresh, but dark, at the edge of my consciousness, perhaps what could have been my last moment, when her face with its headscarf, leaned over me as it was doing now.

"Lying stock-still," she continued in a whisper.

"Like a child," she added, and looked about the room. Her eyes stopped at my trousers that lay in a heap near the bed. At Remek's, which also lay on the floor a few steps from mine. At Remek, who was lying asleep as if he were dead.

I sat up in bed and put on my glasses.

"Please let me explain . . ." I said.

"Shh." She nodded towards where Remek was sleeping, and then looked at me.

"I can imagine what you're thinking . . ." I stuttered.

"I'm not thinking anything," she whispered, hugging her shoulders as if she were cold. She was again wearing her red dress and tight blouse, which left her shoulders and arms bare. Her lips were heavily rouged and almost as red as her dress. Her face was brighter than usual, but washed out, almost transparent, as if she hadn't slept all night either. Or, I thought, perhaps it was only because of the ray of powerful sunlight that was trained on her like a reflector. In any case, all I saw were her lips, floating in the air à la Man Ray, without a face, and above all without eyes.

"What do you mean you're not thinking anything?" I insisted, still staring at her lips.

"Andreas Haas called. The Little Prince," her red lips slowly articulated.

I pulled the covers over my head and peeked at Remek, who still hadn't moved.

"He has a beautiful voice, who would have thought . . . a true baritone."

I let her talk on. How am I going to get up and get dressed, it suddenly occurred to me, glancing at my wet trousers on the floor. Where is my shirt? Where are my shoes? . . . In the Toyota . . . And where is the Toyota? How am I going to get out of this room? How am I going to explain all this to her?

"He wants to come here so he can take you on a trip along the canals of Venice and show you the Palladian villas"

"The Palladian villas?"

"The villas that were built by . . ."

"You're going to explain to me, of all people, who Andrea Palladio is?" I said, raising my voice unnecessarily, and could have added: "To me, who knows Andrea Palladio like the back of my hand, to me, who a few years ago wrote a series of articles for a *Petronius* feature, 'Today's Grandest Villas'?"

Remek mumbled something and rolled onto his stomach. Only his hair, his neck, and one of his shoulders peeked out from under the covers.

Finally she got up and walked about the room. She pushed shut one of the half-open drawers of the dresser, adjusted the shade of the lamp that was standing on it, ran her finger along its edges, and stood still in front of a table not far from the window.

"I've been looking for these everywhere," she exclaimed in disbelief, reaching out for a pair of silver earrings. She pressed them in her palm and again turned towards me. I had managed in the meantime to slip on my damp trousers

"I ought to have guessed I left them here last time."

I did up the last button of my fly. She put on her earrings. We stood so close that I could hear her breathe.

"Tomorrow I'm going to Ljubljana," her lips said, quietly, suddenly colourlessly.

64

Go on, ask me what town I shall never visit again!

What grim town hides behind such a tender name?

How can such a constricted town have such a long and empty high street?

What can a person do on an interminable afternoon in high summer in this town?

How does this same person feel, walking up and down through this same town on this afternoon that simply will not end, during a high summer that despite everything is coming to an end, as everything is coming to an end, nobody talking to him, nobody looking him in the eye, nobody well-disposed towards him?

Ask me what it was I was doing in such a town!

Ask me if it is possible for a person to be infected by indifference and egoism!

Ask me how one dies there . . .

65

As you can see, I did not go to Venice to float slowly along the canals with Haas, gazing at Villa Godi, Villa Piovene, Villa Forni-Cerato, Villa Gazzoti, Pisani, Saraceno, Thiene, Poiana, or Villa Sarego. We did not spend the night in the left wing of the Villa Emo, nor the following day did we walk silently through the fields of wheat to the Villa Rotonda, my favourite.

"What happened?" Haas asked me over the phone.

That's a good question, what had happened? – I wondered, closing my eyes and trying to impose some order on my thoughts. But every time I closed my eyes, trying to clarify things, I only saw a deepening darkness before me, rent here and there for a few seconds by violent light. And then Lejka's face, as if the violence of the night and that face were one. How innocently you sleep, she had said, mocking and serious at the same time, as if that were the only phrase we would ever be able to utter about what had happened.

"Nothing," I told Haas, the way Lejka did when something *was* happening.

"Where are you?" he asked, increasingly impatient.

My eyes panned into a slow panoramic shot. A colour picture of snow-covered mountains with a lake below. A pale green wall. The television playing without the sound on. An open bathroom door. A window looking out onto the courtyard. A table. An open bottle of Union beer. A chair. A checked bedcover.

"In my hotel room," I replied.

"What are you doing in a hotel?" he continued.

"Sleeping," I said, as if it were self-explanatory, which it wasn't. I hadn't managed to close an eye in this room.

"Alone?"

"Yes, alone," I repeated, adding with a touch of coquetry, "For the time being."

"Are you serious?"

"Nope," I said, laughing, which wasn't true either.

"What about the Slovenian?" he asked.

I exhaled slowly, as if I were doing breathing exercises. What should I tell him about Lejka, I thought, and slowly inhaled. That she had left in the night, that she had gone with Ingrid to Ljubljana? That she had let herself be talked into it? . . . Or that she had been incapable of saying no, or that it was actually what she had wanted? . . . To go back home for a few days, she had said the morning after the storm, as we sat in her Toyota on our way back to Sežana. Home to mama, to Ingrid. It has been such a long time since I've been home, she said. In my room, my old room . . . I don't even remember the smell . . . Of my room, of the flat, of Ljubljana . . . Are you sure that's a good idea, I asked, as if I had known in advance that it was in fact the worst possible idea. I am sure, she had said, more to herself than to me, and added that in a few days Ingrid was to give one of her summer lectures on medicinal and poisonous plants. No, this time only on poisonous plants. Poisonous plants that can also heal, or something like that, she said. In short, Ingrid would love to have her daughter attend her lecture on poisonous plants. And Lejka had

141

accepted. How was it possible, I exclaimed, also more to myself than to her. How was it possible that she would attend a lecture on some silly plants while her mother, God knows why, simply wouldn't come to see her on stage? How was it possible that we were heading precisely for the one place we didn't want to go? But Lejka interpreted my outburst in her own fashion. Of course you're coming with me, she said, as if it had all been arranged. Don't worry, I won't leave you alone here in Sežana, she said with a side-long glance, and laughed for the first time that morning. Which I also interpreted in my own fashion. She doesn't want to leave us alone together, I thought. Remek and me, I mean . . . who else?

"The Slovenian is back home under her mother's wing," I replied.

66

Of course she loved Ljubljana – what a question! I'd even say she loved it more than your poetess, long-distance runner, social worker, and your television celebrity all put together. What I should really say is that she loved Ljubljana desperately, despite everything, in other words more than those who love it complacently (if I may put it that way) or out of habit – because they have no choice.

The first few days, I myself tried hard to work up some enthusiasm. I walked all over town, trying to educate myself about Plečnik's architecture as quickly as I could. Had I not been secretly hoping that Julijan Remek would come to see me while he was competing in the National Archery Championship, I would have asked dejected Haas (more and more the Little Prince) to come to Ljubljana, exchanging Andrea Palladio for Jože Plečnik: A somewhat mannered Renaissance neoclassicism for neoclassicism *tout court*, yet also somewhat mannered. Exchanging one interpretation of the column – massively antique – for another – ascetically elegant. Exchanging one man's vision – permissively antique – for that of another – spiritually Catholic. "Come on, show a little originality," I would have said to Haas, suggesting that he hop on the first plane to Ljubljana. I had begun writing a piece for *Petronius* called "The Discreet Charm of Proviniciality". I had tried to close my eyes to the parvenu luxury cars rivalling one another on the streets of Ljubljana. And to their parvenu owners, parading about on café terraces and in expensive restaurants in unbelievably parvenu outfits. "Damiani Boutique comes to Ljubljana!" the newspapers announced. I tried to close my eyes to the unbelievable shop windows and their equally unbelievable signs. To the just as unbelievable (not to use a stronger adjective) TV programmes. Or to the fragment of some retrograde, naïve Slovenian film where I didn't have to turn off the sound since none of the actors ever opened their mouths. I tried to see only the beautiful, young faces. The bright smiles. The way in which they moved, laughed, kissed, carefree, extravagant, as if nothing in this world ever came to an end. The graffiti on the banks of the river that runs indifferently through the town. The banks of that same slow river with their unkempt weeping willows. The path leading up to the castle above the town.

The damp streets leading down from it. The market with its fish stalls. The Tivoli Park with the colonnade by Plečnik, particularly at nightfall when the lamps are lit. The *Trg francoske revolucije* – Square of the French Revolution – with its phallic homage to Napoleon – who'd have thought . . . Even the opera house, like a sugar-coated cake. Even the town cemetery. I drowned myself in the local beer called Union. I bought a whole case of the bright-red cans, and dispersed them about my hotel room. A few times I even bought, quite nonchalantly, a copy of the national newspaper with its sagacious name *Delo*, and leafed through it just as nonchalantly – once, quite miraculously, even falling asleep over it.

"Don't you think Ljubljana has a unique aroma? That it smells like no other city in the world?" Lea Kralj asked me.

"No," I replied, and shook my head.

67

"Why not?" she exclaimed, pushing me forwards. We were walking along that long main street, the former Tito Avenue (as she told me), which now has at least three different names, and leads from one end of town to the other, and which drives me to the brink of depression, as I have already mentioned.

"Madrid is redolent of La Mancha . . . Paris of the *métro*, croissants and *café crème* . . . Milan of canapés and Stendhal . . . And Ljubljana . . . Ljubljana is redolent of . . ."

"Why don't we go back to Sežana?" I cut in.

"Sežana?"

"Back to your place."

"Ljubljana is my place too," she said, suddenly stopping and looking at me. "What's wrong with you? You've changed in the last few days."

"You too," I said with absolute conviction.

We looked at one another for a few moments and then continued walking down the former Tito Avenue in silence. Lea Kralj walked a step ahead of me, though I was trying to catch up with her. It is clear that she has changed, I said to myself. She no longer knows how to walk with me, I mean, in step with me, the two of us next to each other the way we have done till now, regardless where, when, or in what weather – in Paris, Milan, Sežana . . . Suddenly she is in a hurry, suddenly she is impatient, suddenly her voice is sharper. Suddenly she is different.

"Do you want me to take you to have some cakes?" she said, trying to smile at me, as we waited at the main crossing for the lights to change.

"Cakes?"

I was ready to go anywhere, as long as we left this ominous street that used to be Tito Avenue.

When we were sitting in the Slon Café, each in front of a cream puff and a glass of fruit juice, I told myself that it was quite evident that there was something wrong with our first day in Ljubljana. Firstly (and very importantly), we were no longer able to walk in step the way we had before, and that in her home town. Secondly, her home town evidently did not inspire her, as she had not done a single one of her imitation skits, the way she usually did when we walked together in other towns, or when we sat in a café. There was always somebody who would somehow catch her attention and whom she could not resist imitating. Perhaps we are kinder to our compatriots, who knows, or perhaps there was nobody around who drew her notice in any way. Thirdly, and apparently less importantly (though in fact more importantly than I realised at the time): neither of us had touched our cream puffs that lay before us. I was in no mood for this creamy local speciality. And I didn't even wonder why she was not eating. I knew that Lea Kralj had a complicated relationship to food, particularly to desserts. She might not have a proper meal for three days in a row, but stuff herself with waffles or *marrons glacés* between rehearsals. I knew that after a fine lunch or dinner she was capable of fasting so she would not cross the fateful line of nine stone. In short, Lea Kralj would never have become one of those fat, sacerdotal prima donnas who have a sublime voice and portly neck, who cannot bend at the waist, and who the tenors have to kiss from a distance. I did notice that she was somewhat pale, that her collar-bones protruded more than usual, and that her neck seemed longer. Perhaps because she was avoiding my eyes and holding her face to the left or to the right. But surely Madame Ingrid was watching over her and what she ate. Now that she was finally near her and belonged to her alone.

"Ingrid would like to invite you for lunch," she said, as if reading my mind.

68

In order to reply to your question about her close bond to home and family, as you put it, I will have to go back for a bit to the Via Fiori Chiari. To one of those mornings in the kitchen where we were sitting after breakfast at the table with the green stems, before the phone started ringing, while the snow was falling outside and Lea Kralj was laying out all the plans she had for Madame Ingrid's visit: we will take her to the Botanical Gardens, to our Ristorante Verdi, to the shops, we have to buy some cold-pressed virgin olive oil, and some new towels . . . Cleanliness is all-important for Madame Ingrid . . .

"Are you sure?" I asked.

"Of what?"

"That you're not going a bit too far. New towels, and all that."

"No, I'm not going too far," she said, getting up and beginning to pace up and down the kitchen. "And I don't know why you're poking your nose into this. I'm sure you'd do the same for your mother if she came to visit you . . ."

"I wouldn't . . ."

"Stop it, please."

She leaned back against the oven and folded her arms. She was wearing her blue nightgown, a thick pullover, and woollen socks. Her eyelids were still puffy with sleep. She had plaited her hair into a thin, ridiculous braid.

"I really wouldn't. I wouldn't because I don't have a mother."

"What do you mean?"

"My parents were killed in a car crash. It seems my father loved speed. When he bought the car, he still didn't have a licence. For a long time my mother hadn't wanted to get in the car with him. But one day he managed to talk her into it. 'You really don't trust me, Silvia?' he had asked her. They crashed into a plane tree and were dead on the spot . . . I was two-and-a-half and became an orphan in a single afternoon."

"Oh, I'm sorry . . ." she said, turning white, and came up behind me. She hugged my shoulders with both hands, and kept murmuring, "I'm sorry, I'm sorry."

"Don't worry," I said, wriggling out of her embrace. "Sit down here at the table and look at me . . . Yes, like that. Is something missing in my life? Do I look unhappy to you?" I asked, as she sat down on the chair opposite me. "My mother's sister, Anna, became my guardian. She brought me to Paris to live with her. Before that we had lived in Nice, where my parents owned a nightclub. Anna was a seamstress. I used to spend whole days playing near her sewing machine . . . She didn't send me to nursery school or kindergarten . . . she looked after me and loved me as if I were her own child. Perhaps even more . . . I'm certain that it was more . . . She never married, even though she had Marco. 'Had' is not the right word. Marco actually had a family, a real one I mean, a wife, children . . . He came over only from time to time, usually in the evening . . . an incredible man . . . he was a foreman at Citroën, but very elegant, always in a white shirt . . . Once we all went for a few days to the seaside, only once. Marco carried me on his shoulders, Anna had sewn

148

me some shorts and a funny little sunhat ... Everybody thought we were a real family ... A real father, a real mother, a real son ... I usually called Anna 'Anna' or 'Auntie Anna' ... Or 'Annette' ... 'Annette', when something had made her angry, when her clients didn't pay her or when she was sad for some reason ... But at the seaside, in Brittany, I called her 'mama'. I was without a family, but happy, believe me. Not a single family problem. Free. Alone in the world ... What could be better?" I proclaimed, and sighed deeply.

We sat in silence for a while.

"If you think about it, I don't have a family either," she said. "A real family ... even though I'm always doing my best to have one ... I suppose I am frightened of not being from anywhere ... belonging to no-one," she added. She rested her forehead on the green stems and burst out laughing, yes, burst out laughing.

69

When I saw her room for the first time, the one she had as a child – in fact the last room she had really lived in – I could not believe my eyes. Imagine a square room with a window looking out onto a playground filled with children's voices. Imagine furniture from the early seventies, by definition bordering on kitsch and bad taste: a narrow bed, a green bedspread with a cube-pattern, a wardrobe, a Formica desk, two armchairs, a cabinet with bookshelves and glass doors that had some sort of design. On the desk was an old Grundig television, clearly only there because nobody had taken it to the rubbish tip. A stack of files and documents. Even some cardboard boxes on and beside the wardrobe. The only beautiful item in the room was an old, early-twentieth-century table lamp with an orange glass shade and bright beads hanging around it.

"That belonged to my grandfather," she said, noticing my eyes alighting on it.

"Have you seen these photographs?" She pointed at a few framed black-and-white pictures on the wall above the bed.

"And my toys?" Some old teddy bears and dolls were stacked on one of the two armchairs.

"I found them in the wardrobe and sat them all next to one another. This bear, the one missing an ear, has . . ."

"Lea," I exclaimed, "this place is a . . . a storeroom."

"What do you mean?"

"Well, take a good look around you."

She sat down on the armchair that was free of toys and stared at the window. I crouched down in front of her. I wanted to take her hands in mine, raise her, drape something over her shoulders even though it wasn't cold (the room was hot and stuffy), and take her away from here, far away, before she could open her mouth and begin to speak.

"Why is it you don't understand?" she said, without looking at me.

"My holidays are almost over, let's go back to Sežana for a few days where everything's nice and peaceful, just you and me," I said, almost begging her.

"You're only thinking of yourself . . . and Remek . . ." she said, still staring at the window.

"I don't know what is happening to you."

"I don't know what is happening to you either," she murmured.

"Food's ready!" came from the kitchen.

At the table I took a look at her family. I had nothing else to do except eat (I still remember what) and look at them, one by one, in the photographs and in real life. Lejka's sister Mili, a molecular biologist, a traditional, tanned beauty. Smaller than Lejka, blond, without the yellowish freckles beneath the eyes, with the same regular features as her mother, and an extremely well-proportioned body in tight, white trousers and an even tighter T-shirt. She wore a small gold cross around her neck. Her wrists tinkled with cheap bracelets. Her nails were wine red. "Do you speak English?" she asked me, and did not address me again throughout the rest of the meal. Her husband, a professor of European Law, with a slight paunch though he was not yet thirty-five, launched into a lecture on the coordination of Slovenia's legislation with that of Europe and its projected entrance into the European Union (not inquiring whether I was the least bit interested in the subject). He cleared his throat after every few sentences, his eyes darting right and left. Their sons – one a miniature copy of his mother, the other of his father – kept kicking each other under the table and vying to be the centre of attention, until Madame Ingrid finally sent them out to the playground. Madame Ingrid, in a new, comfortable dress, her glasses hanging around her neck, was enthroned at the head of the table and was looking at photographs that Mili and her husband had taken at the seaside. She had a comment for each picture, and handed them ceremoniously to Lejka, who obediently took them, looked at them, turned to her sister, was surprised at the pictures, amazed, asked questions, and then reached over the table to pass them to me.

I wondered what was so surprising about these pictures. The two boys splashing about in the sea. Mili sunbathing. The expert in European law wearing a diving mask and fins, his short hairy legs, his paunch. Mili again, sunbathing, shapely. And then a similar series in Slovenia's Julian Alps, but this time everyone wearing hiking garb. What if I showed these people Lejka's pictures – for instance the one with her headscarf on the Place de la Bastille? Or the ones we published in *Petronius*? Or the celebrated picture of her as diva on the cover of her second album?

Every time she handed me one of the photographs, I tried to catch her eye. What are we doing here at this table, pent up in this airless kitchen? What do you have in common with these people? Let's get into your green Toyota, make a dash for my hotel, and get out of this cramped, musty town. Let's just get up, gather our things together, and *adiós señores, adiós* Professor of European Law, romping little boys, and pretty Mili . . . And of course, Madame Ingrid – forgive me, I should have started with you. Mothers are always first and last. Well, what's done is done, so, once again, thank you for everything and . . . But Lejka didn't hear me. The more I tried to convince her, the more distant she became. She sat clasping her upper arms and looking straight through me. Next to Mili, she seemed unhealthily pale, almost transparent.

When we were sitting in front of our empty coffee cups, I had no other choice but to get up. Alone. I thanked everybody: Ingrid, Mili, the professor, Lejka . . . Lejka didn't move. Ingrid walked me through the long corridor to the door. She clasped my wrists with both hands, as if this were a final farewell. Goodbye, she said, and let the heavy door fall shut behind me.

70

"What's going on?" Haas asked me again on the phone. His voice sounded worried. It has been such a long time since we have seen each other, I thought, trying to remember when it was.

"Nothing," I replied, and that with complete seriousness.

"What do you mean 'nothing'?" he said with surprise, as if he did not believe me but really wanted to.

"I have been taking a nap. In a hotel called Mrak – *mrak* means 'dusk'. I am watching television with the sound off. I am eating whatever I can get my hands on. I am drinking. A fruit juice called 'Fructal' and especially a beer called 'Union'. I have been going for walks all over town . . . Towards evening I will either head for Tivoli Park or the river . . . where it's teeming with bars."

I could have added: I am waiting . . . for Remek, and also for her, the Slovenian.

"Alone?" he asked, more quietly, and no doubt running his hand over his neck. When he is feeling embarrassed he tends to run his palm over his neck. I could see him with his phone walking up and down his bright living room, over the varnished Scandinavian parquet (his flat smells of pale, Scandinavian forests and Polish vodka, of which he always has a bottle in his freezer). I could see him stop in front of the door to the bedroom and lean against the doorframe with his lower back, one foot against the frame . . . Holding the phone with one hand, massaging his neck with the other.

"Alone," I said as convincingly as possible.

I heard him cross the threshold into the bedroom and let himself drop down on his low bed with its velvet counterpane.

"How long have you been in lovely Ljubljana?" he asked warily, as if not expecting a reply. His fingers drummed on the enormous bed. "What about the Slovenian? Is she back at home under her mother's wing?"

"More than ever," I said, even though I would have been far happier had I been able to give a different response. For example, that everything had come to an end: the holiday at Ingrid's in the yellow block of flats not far from the river, Ingrid's triumphant smile, Lejka's room, the beef broth, the roast potatoes, the family photographs from the seaside and the mountains, the lectures on medicinal and poisonous plants . . . After all, Ljubljana is a bit of a hole, charming, but a hole.

"Are you sure you don't want me to come and get you? I could reserve room seventeen in the Villa Emo, the room in the left tower with the view of the cypress trees and the magnolias," he said, surely rolling onto his stomach.

71

Have you come to say goodbye?" Madame Ingrid asked, looking me up and down as I stood at the door of her flat.

She led me through the long corridor to the kitchen.

"Sit down. I'll see if she's awake," she said, also sitting down at the table. She lit a cigarette and drew in a first, deep mouthful of smoke.

"With her you never know when she wants to sleep, when she wants to eat, when she wants to play the piano . . . But you know her well enough . . . she has no sense of order whatsoever . . . as if she were still in a hotel . . . though even in a hotel you can't just eat whenever you're in the mood, don't you think?" she said, waiting for me to agree. "Would you like me to make you some coffee?" she added. "Or some herbal tea . . . a nice slice of cake, freshly baked?"

I resolutely shook my head, and turned and looked at the door.

"So the holidays have come to an end . . . sooner or later everything comes to an end," she said.

I didn't know whether I should agree with this bit of wisdom or not. I got up and headed for Lejka's room.

"Wait," Madame Ingrid called out after me.

She knocked on Lejka's door and opened it without waiting. I heard her say a few short Slovenian sentences (I couldn't tell if they were benevolent or not), close the window, and put some things on the desk.

"What did I tell you?" she said with a conspiratorial smile as she came out of the room.

My prima donna was sitting on her bed. She had pulled her legs up to her chin and was hugging them with both hands as if she were cold. She was wearing the print dress she had worn in Paris and which she was also wearing in

155

the photograph on the Place de la Bastille, though it can't be seen (the dress, I mean). She was made up, coiffed, ready, as if about to go out. Her white sandals were waiting at the side of the bed.

"I thought you were no longer here . . . that you'd gone," she said.

"Gone where?"

"I don't know. To Temnica, perhaps."

"To Temnica?

"Or to those villas . . . Just now when Remek is coming to Ljubljana for the National Championship, or something like that . . . You see, I am well informed."

"What are you doing in this room?"

"I am pleased you didn't leave."

"Really?"

"Really. This morning I thought we could go out dancing together . . . dancing in Ljubljana. What do you say to that? We've never been out dancing together . . . You know how to dance, don't you?"

"Let's go," I said.

"Where?"

"Dancing."

"Now?" She looked at me as if she hadn't quite understood. I walked towards her from the door; until that moment I had been leaning against it, looking at her from a distance. It was late morning, the room already smelled stuffy and stale. Next to her on the bed lay some music scores covered with pencil marks.

"Now . . ." she repeated to herself, but in a different voice, as if she had an idea. Then she suddenly got up, pushed the two armchairs against the wardrobe, rolled back the carpet, and turned on the table lamp.

"Here . . ." she said, as she stopped in front of me out of breath, chewing her lower lip. Little drops of sweat had gathered around her eyes. It was only now that I saw that the print dress which in Paris had clung tightly to her waist and hips was hanging from her like a sack.

"What's wrong with you?" I whispered. I wanted to continue in a single breath: Have you taken a look in the mirror? Look at your bony shoulders and birdlike face. What is going on in this house? What game are we playing? Put on your shoes, take your bag, and let's get out of here . . . We'll dance together some other time, and definitely some other place . . .

"Shh!" she interrupted after my first sentence and grabbed hold of my hand. She put her arm around my waist and waited for me, willy-nilly, to do the same. Then she began. First in a whisper, then la-la-la . . . in a faster dance-rhythm, which at first I didn't recognise. Then her fluttering *Kaj jo je prignalo, od kod je le prišla čisto noter vate jokat lastovka* . . . And then louder and louder, one, two, three, between bed, wardrobe, and desk, one, two, three . . . I felt her voice rise between us, rise up from below, from near the uterus and ovaries, as she had once told me. Suddenly I no longer thought of what I had wanted to tell her just half a minute ago, the stuffy room, her voluntary prison, her thin face, not to mention Madame Ingrid . . . that all she needed to do was open the door and leave. I thought of something entirely different, even though I wasn't thinking any more, as I had abandoned myself completely to her voice. I only told myself that surely nobody had heard Lea Kralj sing from so close up, regardless of what Toronto might say or write. From so close it is something completely different, physical, perhaps even sexual, yes, sexual.

At that moment the door was flung wide open. Ingrid looked at us and said something brusque and sharp, even though a smile flashed over her face.

"It's true . . ." Lejka replied with unexpected sweetness. "I forgot that I mustn't sing in this flat. I can play the piano. But I mustn't sing. Or vocalise. What would the neighbours say?"

72

If I could do it again . . . My amiable weakness . . . My cherished mania . . . My sweet hypocrisy . . . The leitmotiv that helps me live . . . Some people go to confession. Others abandon themselves to different manias: work, sex, a hunger for power . . . Others forget themselves in alcohol . . . I say to myself: If I could do it again . . . My memory always retraces its steps . . . Slowly, carefully . . . One step after another . . . Millimetre by millimetre . . . Right back to that point beyond which there is no return . . . As if I were playing a film backwards, pressing rewind, stopping at the precise movement, word, action where it all went wrong, believing with conviction that now I could put everything right again.

If I could do it again, I would dance once more with

Lea Kralj, even if only in her old room between her bed, wardrobe, and desk. I would let her grab hold of my hand again . . . and above all immerse myself in her voice, in that powerful stream that rose between us, my eyes once again clouding over, my pubic region tightening. And when Madame Ingrid would open the door and utter those sharp sentences, I would take her by the hand – Lejka, I mean. That's enough! – I would say to Madame Ingrid – Enough abuse! Enough torture, enough anger, enough sugary malice! . . . With my other hand I would snatch up Lejka's sandals and drag her out of the room. If she hesitated or resisted in any way, I would lift her up in my arms or somehow get her to the long corridor. I would open the door and drag her to the stairs . . . Outside I would hold her hand even tighter and continue dragging her behind me. To the river and then straight on past the chestnut trees, straight on . . . I would drag her as if they were hot on our heels, even if she flailed about, tripped, fell, shouted . . . I would simply grab her wrist even harder . . . Not till we got to the other side of the bridge would I let go of her, would I let her catch her breath. *Ali si nor, čisto nor,* she would gasp at the end of her strength, and sit down on the ground.

I was '*nor*' – mad . . . Or rather not mad enough . . . Be that as it may, I can press rewind as often as I like, but the fact remains that Lea Kralj stayed in her old room, sat down on the bed again, and looked at me as if to say: "Don't go away . . . please . . . don't leave me alone"; and that I still walked down the long corridor and let the heavy door fall shut behind me.

73

The National Archery Championship? Nobody knew a thing about it – it was as if I had said "Ming Period pottery, or pedigree rabbit breeding". Not to mention that I was already getting strange looks at the hotel. Finally I did find someone among the hotel guests who made a few phone calls and then ten minutes later managed to give me some information: Bus number five to the last stop, and then ask someone there – they'll know.

So I got on bus number five. I looked around – faces and the long road, a tad more picaresque than the former Tito Avenue – and tried to think up additional reasons why I would attend the National Archery Championship. Imagine one of my close friends – not even Haas – asking me not only what I was doing in Ljubljana, but also what in God's name I was doing on bus number five. I could present it as some sort of defiance, a challenge, as an excellent example of going 'against the grain'. Why not be in Ljubljana, the slow-beating heart of that tiny terra incognita, though just a stone's throw away from Venice or Vienna? Why not be on bus number five with the unknown faces, not less unknown after all than the faces on my Parisian bus number thirty-one? Why not ride through the sleepy provincial town on that humid Sunday morning? Why not that hilly, tedious suburb? And why not archery, the discipline *par excellence* that combines spirit and body, earth and sky, oneself and the target?

When I got off the bus at the last stop with one other

passenger, and he showed me the way to the nearby woods that had some sort of clearing where the National Archery Championship was to take place, I was far from exhausting my defiant reasons for being here. I walked along a path that led past a huddled group of houses to the woods.

Why not an archer named Julijan Remek? – I asked myself, studying the faces from a distance and trying to make my way through the crowd of fans and spectators – Why not the best and most handsome of them all? "R" like a grinding mill. In front – between your teeth . . . And the stress on the first syllable . . . *Re*-mek, whom I had seen for the first time through the window of the green railway carriage, with whom we drove about in the light-green Toyota, crossed the border, listened to the programme of Radio Slovenia 3, painted the walls in the upstairs room of Lejka's house in Sežana, each his own wall, each next to the other, while Lea Kralj sang Cavaradossi's "E lucevan le stelle ed olezzava la terra" . . . with whom we had conspiratorially worn the white clothes for a few days longer and had sported the white spots on our hands and were happy. The young man living at the edge of a village with the ominous name of Temnica – "dungeon" – alone in a big house that was empty, almost frightening, as Lejka had said, still waiting for his parents to return from the madhouse where a few years earlier his mother had been taken, his father following her voluntarily . . . The customs officer who, when his parents lost their minds, escaped to his meadow, bought a bow, set up some targets, drew into himself the peace and immovability of the mountains, and taught himself to see the target not just with his eyes . . . The first archer I ever met and went to watch on his meadow, who never let himself be disturbed, and with whom – O tension of tensions – I shot my only arrow without seeing or knowing where it landed. The lover of Lea Kralj, Julijan, Remek, with whom I spent the stormiest night of my life.

Why not him and his sweet *ricardo* (in spite of Lea Kralj), I kept repeating as I searched among the unknown bodies and faces. I made a wide arc through the woods to get to the other side where the targets were.

Why not another stormy night, water streaming down and the sky raging, the sudden shards of light and the moaning of the wind? And after that unrepeatable night, a new, new-born morning, quiet and wordless . . . What could we say to one another after such a ferocious night, I was telling myself in encouragement, when I heard rapid footsteps behind me.

By the time I turned around to see what the rustling leaves and the muffled voices meant, it was already too late. I felt a pain in my stomach and blood ran from my nose.

74

"But what in God's name happened?" Haas asked me one last time.

I propped myself up in bed and leaned my head against the wall, which was pleasantly cool. I touched my chin, still swollen and painful, my nose that was in its place, and closed my eyes. In the past few days I had managed to endure this hotel room only with difficulty, even though I had put the picture of the snow-covered mountains and the lake beneath my bed, and the checked bedspread in the wardrobe.

"Have you lost your voice?" he asked impatiently.

"No . . . I lost my watch . . . my fountain-pen . . . my notebook . . . my Zippo . . . my wallet, of course . . . and . . . and . . . my glasses," I finally uttered. "I have my glasses, but they're broken . . . one of the lenses, the other . . ."

"How about telling me everything from the beginning?" he almost pleaded.

"What beginning?" I said, genuinely taken aback. For a moment I didn't know what beginning he meant – Madrid, Sežana, Ljubljana?

"What were you doing in the woods? And outside town?" he asked with growing impatience.

"Nothing," I replied, shaking my head.

"Are you making fun of me?" he asked, desperate.

"No, no . . ." After a few long moments I again shook my head. I only wanted to say that I really wasn't doing anything in the woods, that he knew me well enough to know that I wasn't the bucolic type, that I was only trying to get to the other side of the clearing, to the targets, and that two men had jumped me from the bushes, punched me in the stomach and face, emptied my pockets, and had run off as suddenly as they had appeared. Nothing extravagant. The same thing had almost happened to me somewhat earlier just a few streets away, in broad daylight. It was just that I didn't return on bus number five, riding through an unknown town to a shadowy hotel with a shadowy name, and supposedly waited for the matter with the Slovenian prima donna somehow to end.

"Are you alone?" Haas asked.

"Yes."

"What about the Slovenian?"

"I don't know."

75

It might sound incredible, but I really didn't know. I would say that nobody can know what really happened in those final days behind the synthetic curtain on the fourth floor of the yellow block of flats not far from the river. Her last summer in Ljubljana, at the pinnacle of her glory, as you have written. Only a few months after a bouquet of white flowers had been placed every morning at her doorstep in the Via Fiori Chiari . . . Nobody except Madame Ingrid, who of course has her own version of the incidents, the maternal version and the medical, one less reliable than the other. At any rate, they were now finally alone together. Lea Kralj was home at last, with her mother, in her old room. And I, for the first time in my life, dreamt that I was flying. That I was falling, falling, but that I never actually fell, which I suppose meant that I was flying, and perhaps also that I could now leave, that I had no reason for remaining any longer in this town, except to bid a quick goodbye to Lea Kralj

"Close the door," she had said when I entered her room.

Her voice came from a distance, even though she was sitting exactly where she had sat the last time, hugging her legs which were pulled up beneath her chin. Her white sandals were again waiting at the side of her bed.

"What are you looking at?" she asked.

At first I had thought that she was naked. That she was only wearing white cotton socks and her headscarf with the colourful birds, tied beneath her chin. All I could see were her long arms and legs. It was only then that I saw she was wearing a short summer dress with thin straps.

"How handsome you are," she said in a voice that was still faraway.

I continued looking at her. At her bony shoulders and long arms that were no longer soft. At her prominent collarbones. At her long neck and the creases in her cheeks. At her paleness and those incredible, yellowish freckles beneath her eyes, which I could never decide whether they were beautiful or ugly. And above all at her eyes. Her eyes are really the colour of tears, I thought, my throat tightening.

"Why aren't you saying anything?" she asked.

"What is wrong with you?" I finally said.

"What do you mean?"

"You're getting thinner every day . . . Soon there'll be nothing left of you! Just take a look at yourself!" I managed to utter with great difficulty.

She laughed into her knees. Then she got up, straightened the straps of her light summer dress, and walked over to the old Grundig television. She bent forward and looked at herself in it as if it were a mirror.

"You're right," she said, shrugging her shoulders as though she were speaking to herself or even interpreting a role. "What do you think this is, a hotel? . . . Where you can eat whenever you want, whenever you're in the mood, the way I do? Of course, when I'm not at my mother's . . . when I'm travelling all over the world, and everybody scrapes and bows – yes, Madame, if you please, Madame. But here at my mother's you eat when she says to, you'd better believe it . . . Or you don't eat . . . Or you stay in your room . . . When you're hungry enough, you're bound to come out . . . Who do you think you are? . . . It's true. Who am I? And what am I doing here? Who can tell me what to do here?"

Then she straightened up and came towards me, so that her whole thin silhouette appeared on the Grundig's dark screen.

"I'm not hungry . . . I'm not hungry . . . Of course I'm hungry . . . How can I not be hungry? . . . But she should come and get me . . . She should come at least once and get me . . . Once . . . Once . . . Just once," she repeated. Then she suddenly burst into tears and collapsed.

I just stood there, like a spectator, unable to move or utter a single word.

"Sorry . . . I've just noticed that you're not wearing your glasses," she said suddenly in a voice that was completely changed, and came even closer. "You look quite different without glasses . . . who'd have thought." She looked at me as if this were the first time she had discovered my real face.

"I have to tell you about Remek," I said on the spur of the moment.

She suddenly laughed, and the shine in her eyes faltered dangerously.

"Is there anything you can tell me that I don't already know?"

"Why are you laughing?" I asked, my voice increasingly pale.

"Remek was for you . . . "

She suddenly became serious.

"What do you mean for me?"

"Do I always have to paint you a picture?" she said softly, resting her hand on my shoulder. "Have you forgotten? The Christmas tree? The Golden Fish, no, not fish . . . fairy, the good fairy?"

I heard myself breathing through my mouth, and continued looking at her. Then she embraced me, both hands tightly hugging my shoulders, and whispered into my ear: "Now leave me alone. My mother will be back any minute. I think she went to the market to buy food for lunch. And you do get on her nerves a bit . . ."

"Lejka . . ."

"*Ciao bello*," she said, pushing me towards the door.

76

A diva? Hardly. Lea Kralj was not a diva, at least not in the sense you mean. Your television celebrity, whom I happened to see on the milky screen in my hotel room (at least I think she was the TV star I saw, who does seem to have every chance of becoming Slovenia's Woman of the Year, no, not year, century), your television celebrity is much more of a diva than Lea Kralj. If for no other reason than because she thinks she is a diva – look how piously she crosses her arms over her breasts, as if she had to protect something God knows how priceless – a thing you really couldn't say about Lea Kralj. Lea Kralj was a diva, a real diva, only once, and that for just a second, and, you could say, by mistake.

She was being photographed for the cover of her second album. François, the photographer's name was François. A small fellow, half a head shorter than Lea, nimble, with round, piercing eyes. She had been dressed in a magnificent gown. Christian Lacroix, if I'm not mistaken. Red, a low décolleté, billowing . . . The make-up artist had made her up heavily, particularly her mouth. The only piece of jewellery Lea Kralj was wearing was a large bracelet with coloured crystals, which had arrived with the dress. I want you to be a diva, as much of a diva as possible, François had said as he danced around her with his heavy equipment. They tried everything. Sitting, standing, shooting in profile, shooting from above, shooting from below . . . "Be a diva for me, just for me, a diva like no other," he coaxed her.

"Do you even know what a diva is?" he finally said, growing desperate.

In the end, she slumped down on the chair. She leaned forward, her dress puffing out even more luxuriantly around her, her breasts rounding out seductively, one hand slipping between her legs, so that it disappeared, sweetly ambiguous, in the red cloth, the other hand poised on her knee, her bracelet almost slipping from her wrist. She threw a sidelong glance at François, haughty, weary, absent, her lips parted as if to say, "Leave me in peace, I want to be alone." François pressed the shutter. And he got his photograph of the diva. The first and last.

77

She was not exhausted. I think it is high time that all this claptrap be swept away: that she was exhausted, that her nerves were at an end, that she was squeezed dry like a lemon. It's not surprising that things ended as they did. Who would not have been exhausted after a season like the one Lea Kralj had behind her, Lluis Toronto had declared, and along with him everyone else. Given half a chance, he would have set up a press conference. The death of the Slovenian Prima Donna! He would have even sported a new suit for the occasion. Lluis Toronto is always dressed to the nines. Even during the most intense rehearsals he will wear bespoke suits: a jacket with three buttons, cuffed trousers, and the obligatory black cotton T-shirt. Not to mention the inevitable pencil in his top right pocket. Have I already mentioned his famous pencil? A pencil brings with it undreamed-of possibilities. You can chew on it, twirl it between your fingers like a cigarette, place it behind your ear, scratch your head with it, beat rhythm, improvise a sword duel, throw it on the floor in a fit of anger, or break it in two – you can even write with it. The conductor has his baton, Toronto his pencil.

If you approach Toronto, he will be ready enough to answer all your questions. You must remember that Lea Kralj was his trophy, his diva. It was he, Toronto, who a week before the première in Madrid had pulled her out of his hat. "Pulled her out of his hat" is perhaps not the right expression. He suggested her to the conductor and the director of the opera, or better yet forced them, twisted their arms into having the stand-in replace the prima donna – can you imagine? It was three years ago at the Zarzuela in Madrid. Right from the beginning, from the first rehearsals with the orchestra, he had noticed that his eyes were always drawn to her, to the stand-in behind the curtain, that it was the first time he had seen such a thing, a singer who did not distort her face while singing – no grimace, no mouth wide open like a toad – a singer who really acted. No waving of arms, no raising of eyes to the heavens. A singer who acted, living and dying at the end as only an Angelica could live and die . . . It was he, Lluis Toronto, who had discovered her natural, powerful voice and also her incredible dramatic talent, her outstanding acting ability, and above all her gift of dying.

No-one knows how to die on stage like Lea Kralj, he repeated at every opportunity. Just remember her Angelica, her Katya, and even her Tosca. Angelica collapsed, despite Puccini's angelic apotheosis, despite the promise of light after darkness, as dying is being alone and then no longer being . . . Katya fell into the water as if she finally wanted to breathe freely, finally rest, finally be at peace . . . And Floria Tosca did not throw herself off the Castel Sant'Angelo, the way all the Toscas on all opera stages do. Lea Kralj stabbed herself with a dagger that she snatched from one of the guards. Theatrical, of course: Floria Tosca is an actress, Floria Tosca wants to die on stage, in full view, as if to say: Look, take a good look, feast your eyes, it is I who will be in pain, the blood that will spill on the ground will be mine. All of you will continue seeing the sun and the clouds and the moon, but I will no longer be . . . The audience held their breath . . . Anyway, Toronto has written it all down. His famous notes, or rather *carnets de bord*. Feel free to ask any questions, ladies and gentlemen . . .

But what could Lluis Puig Xirinacs tell you about Lea Kralj's final days in Ljubljana? About Madame Ingrid? About Lea Kralj's old room? About its furniture, the wardrobe of light veneer, two armchairs, and the Formica desk. About the old Grundig television? Or the framed black-and-white photographs on the wall? Particularly one of them – Lejka in a white coat against a white background, or rather on a snow-covered field through which she is pulling a sledge, only her face and the long rope visible. Perhaps that photograph was taken during the harsh winter in which Madame Ingrid took her daughters to a nearby hill where it was so cold that Lea Kralj never forgot her numb hands. What can we say about that distant memory, about the dark interior of her mother's mouth, and the sick desire of Lea Kralj to disappear for ever in it?

78

All and nothing . . . So I kept postponing my departure from one day to the next, went on walking from one end of Ljubljana to the other, and slept in Hotel Mrak. I went on buying Union beer and, from time to time, the newspaper *Delo*. I masochistically watched local television. Since our last telephone conversation I hadn't heard a peep from my tall, Batavian Lieutenant-Colonel Haas. I sent a postcard of Ljubljana to the editorial office of *Petronius*, on which I wrote – God help me! – that I had caught Hepatitis

B (initially I had written C, but then changed it to B, though I don't know the difference. Anyway, B somehow seemed more plausible). And I wrote that I would fly back the instant I felt a little better: "By the time the sluggish postal service delivers this card to you, I will surely be up and about again – I might well make my appearance within a matter of hours after you get this card. I am letting my feature 'The Discreet Charm of Provinciality' seep into me like a herbal infusion. As it is, all I'm doing here in Ljubljana is waiting," I also wrote, the only line on the card that had some truth in it.

I had never experienced anything like this before . . . Waiting for something to happen, whether good or bad, but just waiting for something to occur, to conclude, to end. Moving neither forwards nor backwards, just as the Ljubljanica River meanders through Ljubljana, as if I were intentionally setting barriers for myself. Being alone not because I wanted to be alone but because I had no other choice. Breathing only from the uppermost region of my lungs. Looking out of the window at the long street that used to be Tito Avenue, the buses, the cars, the people buying bread and milk, the people in the laundrette across the street or in the bar beneath me, many people in the bar beneath me, children bicycling around Napoleon's *ricardo*, cats chasing one another over rooftops . . . I had never before been so sick of the incessant teeming of life. Staring for hours and hours at the net of torn clouds as they changed the pattern of the sky before my eyes. Seeing the same bracing mountains every day with their proud peaks, similar to the ones in the picture I had shoved under my bed in a futile attempt to banish them from sight. Feeling the stagnation of air – also in our hearts.

79

I had never had such dreams before – if I might add that about myself, or rather about my lethargy, which was growing more obstinate every day. And I don't only mean the dreams where I was flying, and where I realised quickly enough that I wasn't actually flying. That in reality I was falling, further every night, that the ground was coming dangerously close and that the only choice I had was the spot on which I would crash. I dreamed about totally unimportant and unconnected actions and incidents, but always with an unusual combination of characters. I would be sitting at the same table with Lea Kralj, Aunt Anna, Pablo and Madame Kudelka, whom I had never seen before. I think it was in a restaurant. Anyway, there were waiters around, and above us the ceiling was covered with frescos. We were sitting in front of our empty plates, waiting. Lejka was talking with Anna, who had a cold and kept slipping her handkerchief into her sleeve, as was her habit. I was sitting next to Madame Kudelka. She was the only one of us whose plate was full. She was chewing something hard, and only nodded or shook her head in response to my questions. She was an elderly lady dressed in black, wearing little, round glasses that had a light tortoiseshell frame similar to mine, and with hair that was white as snow and plaited into two stiff braids that hung down to her breasts. In fact she was quite stout, perhaps not a Montserrat Caballé, but near enough. Pablo had a book in front of him and was reading. The moment I least expected it, Madame Kudelka put down her knife and fork, wiped her mouth, turned to me, and uttered a long sentence of which I didn't understand a single word. She got up and left us without a goodbye. "What did she say?" I asked Pablo. "To give her a kiss from her," Pablo replied, "and to tell her to dress more warmly." "To give a kiss to whom?" "To *la petite*," he replied, nodding towards Lejka.

In other dreams Lea was playing the piano. I was rapping on the front door of Haas's flat. I was beginning to doubt that anyone was there when he finally opened the door. "Are you trying to break down the door? What a ruffian you are!" he whispered. "Can't you hear she's playing?" "Who's playing?" I asked, and only then heard the sound of the piano. I walked in the direction of the sound as if it were a path through a forest. I don't remember Haas's flat being so spacious, I thought, as I walked from room to room, into a long corridor, and then down it. Nor do I remember him having a piano. Finally I saw her across Haas's long living room, sitting at a large concert grand. Lea Kralj, in an orange dress with a small V on her chest, and the headscarf with the birds, which she wore tied at the nape of her neck. Remek was sitting next to her in a white shirt with rolled-up sleeves, carefully following the score and turning the pages for her. "What is she playing?" I whispered to Haas, who was standing behind me. "Can't you guess?" Remek replied, turning a page. "Scherzo no. 2 in B minor, opus 31."

And another time, in other dreams, she was topless in the kitchen. I don't know in which kitchen. In the Via Fiori

Chiari, or in Sežana, or even in mine. In any case, she was leaning against the oven. She was holding a kitchen towel. Her breasts were not large, or small, neither apple-like, nor pear-like. They were like a face, and it was as if they were looking at me. Do you want me to warm your hands, I asked her.

I ran past Napoleon's obelisk, the Square of the French Revolution, and down a narrow alley to the Ljubljanica River, over a bridge, and continued along the river – this not in my dreams, but in reality, although I have often thought that Ljubljana itself was part of my absurd dreams – and I stopped at the playground in front of the yellow block of flats. I wanted to tell her that I had dreamt about Madame Kudelka and to ask if she really looked like a Montserrat Caballé with thin, white braids, wore glasses like mine, and exuded great benevolence. And perhaps even to kiss Lejka, as Madame Kudelka had told me to do, to kiss *la petite*. After all, I had never kissed her. And I wanted to do that now – not tomorrow, not the day after, when we would each go our own way, me to Paris to the rue Gustave-Doré, and she to God knows where . . . As long as we left this place, *adiós señores, adiós.*

A thin curtain hung across her window. Her grand-father's lamp was burning in her room, even though it was day. Needless to say, from where I stood I couldn't see anything. The most I could hope for was her silhouette, should she happen to pass by the window. But no silhouette passed by the window. Except for the orange glow, there was no sign of life behind the curtain. I did not know what to think. Then I saw her sister Mili on the pavement in front of the entrance. She was carrying a plastic bag and went inside. I sighed. What was I thinking? Mili, pretty Mili, would surely stand by her. Those closest to us will not do us harm.

"*Ali je kaj narobe?*" I heard the pleasant voice of an old woman wearing a kerchief who was leaning on a walking stick and looking me up and down.

"*Narobe,*" I said uncomprehending, nodding and smiling at her foolishly.

80

Something of this sort had happened before . . . escape . . . off the air . . . static on the screen . . . not I . . . not Ljubljana . . . tomorrow I will be righteous and bold. Except that this time there was nothing to reconstruct . . . Nobody paid any attention to me . . . Nobody drew me into conversation . . . Nobody leaned over me . . . Not even when my cocktail of sleeping pills and alcohol finally imploded . . . When I began to slip slowly out of myself . . . When I no longer asked myself what in God's name I was doing here in Ljubljana . . . In this bar by the river where I do not know anyone . . . Why did I come to bury myself in this hole that is synonymous with lethargy, agony . . . And what is going on with her, with Lea Kralj, my prima donna . . . Why has she so cruelly left me to myself . . . What is the meaning of these little games . . . Not even when I ended up staring blindly before me . . . When at the door of the bar . . . I no longer know which one . . . I had walked a

few steps forward . . . And then a few more . . . When I
had bumped into someone . . . a man or a woman . . . When
I had grabbed hold of something cold and metallic . . .
When the night became impenetrably thick with twinkling
stars . . . When the cold, metallic object eluded me . . .
When I tried to grab hold of it again . . . To grab hold of
it at all costs . . . But it did not want me . . . No-one wanted
me, quite simply . . . I collapsed on the pavement.

Our blood-group is B-positive, I whispered . . . The
Ljubljanica River with its indistinct colour and indistinct
course flowed past indistinctly . . . Our blood-group is
B-positive, I repeated more loudly . . . Our blood-group
is B-positive, I shouted . . . Someone threw me a sidelong
glance . . . I was under the impression that he said: "*Ali si
nor . . . Čisto nor?*" And if I am mistaken, if he didn't actually say, "Are you mad . . . completely mad?" then I am
sure he thought something of the kind.

I looked into the darkness above me and at the exalted,
unreachable stars . . . Perhaps one of them . . . just one of
them, might notice me . . . Put a scarf on its head and lean
over me . . . at this extreme moment . . . at the edge of
consciousness . . . Lean over me as if to cover me with a
blanket . . .

81

There are only three, no, four of your questions left that I
intend to answer, having answered all the rest, though I
would actually prefer to end here. If I could, if what

happened had not happened, if we hadn't reached the last stop of our journey, I would have ended with the above sentence about the stars. And about one star, which at some point – a long time ago now – had actually worn a head-scarf and leaned over me, as if to cover me with a blanket. But that had been in Madrid. In Ljubljana they looked at me from far away, infinitely exalted and unreachable. Then they did not even look at me any more. They suddenly expired, withdrew from the scene, left, end of performance. After that I do not remember anything. Everything becomes bland, constricted – not dark, but colourless. My Ljubljana amnesia was colourless.

When I opened my eyes, I saw Andreas Haas. My glasses, where are my glasses, I thought. My head was filled with shards. If I moved, they would cut me, make my membranes bleed. I closed my eyes. I no longer have any glasses, I remembered. Since the National Archery Championship I no longer have glasses. Since the National Archery Championship I see everything in a haze, like through the thin, synthetic curtain across Lejka's window.

I opened my eyes again. And Andreas Haas sat before me again. As if he had fallen from the sky. With his white hair, the golden hairs on his arms, and blue eyes.

"Little Prince . . ." I said, and immediately heard the echo of my words in the depths of my head.

He was bent at the waist, his hands propped on his knees, leaning forward as if his body had discovered the position in which it does not feel its weight. Suddenly he leaned even further forward and I saw him clearly from up close. His face, the unshaven cheeks, and above all, that contrast

178

in him that always surprised me: the sharp lines of his nose, cheekbones, and protruding chin, and the softness, the spaciousness of his eyes. And, of course, the colour of his hair, which gave him the look of a grown-up version of the Little Prince.

"Who would have thought . . ." I said. I wanted to add: Lieutenant-Colonel Haas in Ljubljana, the Little Prince in Hotel Mrak . . . or something along those lines. Even to burst out laughing . . . to touch his knees. For an instant everything seemed so unreal. Everything except the bad taste in my mouth and the shards in my head. But if I did not move, they did not harm me.

"At last," he whispered with a loud sigh. "At last."

"How long have you been here?" I asked.

"Too long," he replied, as if he were hiding something from me.

"How long is too long?"

I was beginning to feel unsettled. He looked at me for a few moments. The curtains were pulled back, and the three lamps were lit.

"Your cocktail of Lexomila, Rohypnola, and alcohol is very effective . . . More than effective . . . I think you're becoming a real specialist . . . Perhaps you can give me the recipe one day . . . " he said, as if he wasn't about to stop

"Help me get to the bathroom," I cut in.

I sat up in bed and propped myself on my knee, all the shards rolling to the other side. Haas helped me get up. I slipped one arm around his waist. Darkness flashed before my eyes, and again the shards moved. This is the dark side of my colourless amnesia, I thought. Everything has its dark side, I told myself. Only a few shuffling steps remained to the bathroom. I half-closed the door and sat down on the toilet. Only now did I see that I was wearing nothing but my shirt.

"We're going back to Paris tomorrow," Haas said from the other side of the door. "Today, actually. I don't know if you've noticed how late it is . . . It's almost day."

"I'm not going."

"Of course you are," he replied in the tone of a mother speaking to a capricious child.

"I'm leaving when she leaves, the Slovenian I mean," I said and got up very slowly.

"She's not leaving."

"What do you mean 'she's not leaving'? Of course she's leaving . . . What is she going to do here in Ljubljana? She's got to get ready for Seville. In September she has to go to Seville. Anyway, it's none of your business . . ."

"Lea Kralj is dead."

I steadied myself on the wall. What had he just said? He opened the door and looked at me.

"At her mother's place . . . From exhaustion, some sort of virus . . . It all happened very quickly."

I slumped down on the floor. The shards cut into me and made my membranes bleed.

"It's not true!"

"I didn't know how to tell you."

"It's not true!"

"Give me your hand."

"I tell you, it's not true . . . She's not dead . . ."

"Give me your hand!"

"She's not dead . . . What virus? They let her die . . . Her mother . . . What do you think, you think she was staying in a hotel? In a hotel you can eat whenever you want, but not at her mother's . . . At her mother's you eat when she says to . . . or you don't eat at all. It's simple, very simple . . ."

"What are you talking about?"

"Or you die of hunger . . . If you're hungry enough, you're bound to come out . . . I'm not hungry."

"What's wrong with you?"

"Of course I'm hungry . . . Who isn't hungry for love? Do you understand?"

"No."

"Do I have to paint you a picture?" I said with my last strength.

Suddenly I felt as if I were falling deeper than the cold bathroom floor, onto a floor that was even harder and colder, and that it was the floor I was trying to avoid in my dreams. And when my face finally hit the ceramic tiles something warm spread from under my fingers, like blood from the shards.

Then I saw Haas's face from very close up, first his protruding chin and spacious eyes, that when I first saw them in the *métro* had reminded me of hospital corridors. He laid his hand on my wrist.

"Why are you holding your ears shut?" he asked so quietly that I barely heard him.

"Because I can hear my heart beating in my ears."

82

All I remember the following day is Slovenia beneath me and Haas's right hand resting on his knee all the way to Paris. Everything else seemed dead, there was no going back. It was early in the morning, and the sky had not been so crystal clear in a long time. Like a low flight over Hong Kong, that is to say a landing that takes you right over the town, during which you can see in detail the teeming life below you, in no way comparable to a landing over Slovenia.

I saw everything. Ljubljana, huddling around its castle, and the indecisive Ljubljanica River that embraces itself with both its arms, the yellow block of flats not far from one of them. The long street that was formerly Tito Avenue, that cannot boast the slightest bit of imagination. Even Napoleon's *ricardo*, triumphantly upright. I saw the little, rounded hills with little churches on top and god-fearing little houses beneath (you must forgive me, but from such a perspective I can only call everything "little"). The highways, roads, and paths branching out in all directions. Meadows and fields like motley-coloured strips of cloth. Woods that are dark green, and many more different kinds of green. I saw exalted mountains with snow-covered peaks, but this time I saw them from above. The lake, whose photograph had hung in my room in the Hotel Mrak, garlanded by a crown of snow-covered mountains. I saw the harsh valleys of the Karst, piled-up stones, tall vines . . . Pine forests, commons, winding roads . . . I saw meadows, many meadows, particularly the one that juts out abruptly into the valley, and behind it a long hedgerow of thorny bushes . . . I saw Sežana and Temnica . . . and of course the sea which cuts into the Bay of Trieste. A little earlier I had seen the invisible border that we had crossed, and even the Trieste railway station . . . Everything lay down there . . . And I wanted to see it all one more time. I knew in advance that all these traits would one day form a single face, and that I had to remember them to the last detail.

83

I think you are wrong. Joy does not dispel sorrow. When I go cycling along the Right Bank of the Seine. Beneath the chestnut trees, past Simón Bolívar, the Pont Alexandre III, the Place de la Concorde . . . When evening approaches but it is not yet evening . . . When we turn into silhouettes . . . Of course the first stars emerge and the thin sickle of the moon rises, and suddenly all the lights on the Place de la Concorde light up as if they had heard me. Then, despite the sudden feeling of splendour, or rather because of it, my silhouette is washed over by dull sorrow.

84

I never went back to Slovenia. Only once, in a sense. I had happened to walk into the Fnac Bookstore in Paris. It was one of the last days of the year, on an afternoon when I found it harder to endure the Pharaonic hysteria surrounding the change of calendar. At such moments, I told myself, it is best to plunge into obscure books and obscure CDs, and "peace in Bosnia" (as Lejka used to say).

So I entered Fnac through the main entrance on the Avenue des Ternes (or the Avenue Niel) and gave myself up to the escalators. On the second floor I wandered around among the thousands of music subjects and titles. Of course I knew that in the section of serious music, under K, or under Janáček or Puccini, I would find the few recordings that Lea Kralj had made. But I had not imagined that on that late afternoon, among the countless faces of customers, window-shoppers, idle onlookers, and the faces on the CD boxes lining the shelves, I would suddenly stop in front of hers. Particularly since I had not been looking for her, and had been looking for nothing more than some fleeting feeling of the diversity of existence. My eyes came, so to speak, eye to eye with hers. Lea Kralj, prima donna. "The shock of the year" was written on a hanging publicity sign.

I looked at her photograph as a diva, slightly different to the one I have already described. I reached for the headphones by a pile of CDs almost at the same moment as a young woman pushing a pram with a baby that peered at us curiously.

"Do you know her?" she asked, nodding towards the picture of Lea Kralj.

"Yes, I do."

The child began wriggling in its pram, wanting his mother to take him out or hold him. But she only pushed the pram back and forth with her foot . . . I did not know whether

I should stay or wander through the moving mass of people until the young mother got tired and left. I put on the earphones anyway.

I remember it as if it were yesterday. Her voice, the voice of Lea Kralj that grabbed me, as though by the neck, dragging me behind it. I didn't even have to close my eyes. I was on that snow-covered hill just outside Ljubljana. Everything was so white that for a long time I could not see anything, for a long time I didn't even know where I was, barely able to distinguish the snow from the foggy sky. Then my eyes slowly got used to the blinding tints. In the distance I could make out the castle with Ljubljana huddling around it, and even the inert river. And in front of me, footprints in the snow. And then in that direction, in the direction of the footprints, very far away, I saw a tiny silhouette. It was moving towards me. Running, to the extent that it is possible to run in deep snow. A small creature wearing something bright. From that distance I could not make out her face. I only saw her hands, which she was holding out in front of her and heard some sort of faraway whimpering in her voice.

She got closer and bigger ... the last few yards she was as tall as me. Lea Kralj in her low-cut, orange dress with straps slanted at an angle that charmingly exposed her soft, bare arms, and with the scarf on her head. She was no longer running. She came up to me as if she were no longer in a hurry, somewhat unsteady in the deep snow. She wasn't whimpering any more either, or moaning, though it was clear that her hands were still frozen. She looked straight at me, as nobody had ever looked at me before. I felt a pain above my pubic region and finally knew what I had to do. And when she was right in front of me, and I could see her grey eyes and those incredible yellowish freckles around them, and I only had to open my arms to press her to me, tightly to me to warm her, of course warm her, she disappeared. Disappeared, or rather, moved into me, and I heard her breath within my chest, my arms hanging uselessly by my side. The snow remained as well as her voice, shuddering a few more times as if hovering in front of her shoulders, and then fell silent. Then the snow disappeared too. The recording had come to an end. I again saw the young mother's foot rocking the pram back and forth, and the child, who was clearly enjoying it and grinning mischievously.

85

I am sure I have forgotten something. I don't have a Felisa who comes to clean my flat and inadvertently moves and sorts my memories. This goes here, this goes there, this we can throw out. This too. And this. And this . . . And that, that we have to keep locked in the drawer, right at the bottom of our memory.

What connection does Felisa have to Lea Kralj and Slovenia's Woman of the Century? None, absolutely none.

Felisa has nothing to do with all this, and the only answer I can give to your final question as I write at this late hour in the night or early morning, who knows, is that I hope Lea Kralj will never, I repeat, never become Slovenia's Woman of the Year – no, not year, century.